Tales
from
Grandma Bo's
Cottage

Tales from Grandma Bo's Cottage

MELINDA SELMYS

vulgata

ISBN 978-0991909810

"Ocean of Sand" first appeared in issue 36 of Dreams and Visions in 2007

"The Exhibition" first appeared on Pseudopod episode 90 in May, 2008

"The Idol's Gilded Eye" first appeared in issue XVIII of Vulgata Magazine in February, 2008

"The Golden Bones of Grandma Bo" first appeared in the 30th anniversary edition of Leading Edge in 2011

"How It Was" was written with Neil Patterson

for Egypt

CONTENTS

• • • • •

THE GOLDEN BONES
OF GRANDMA BO

• • • • •

"Grandma Bo?"

"Yes, Thut"

"Tell me a story about death."

It was, perhaps, an odd request, coming from a six year old boy. One must recall, however, that I was a Metenem child growing up in Ptemya. Already, I had heard rumors that one day I would be taken up to the cave to learn the lesson of Death. Since the older children were forbidden to speak of this ordeal to the younger echelons we had all heard a great deal about it. For example, we knew that you were given nothing to eat until you could feel starvation leeching off your bones and that death was a giant eel with seven heads that stank like rotting fish. I wanted

Grandma Bo to either confirm or deny the part about the giant eel.

"About death?" Grandma Bo laughed. "I will tell you a story about a ghost that used to live on the road north of here."

"Is there Death in it?"

"The ghost is quite dead, as all good ghosts are."

I settled myself, kneeling with my hands placed neatly on my knees. Several of my Suese cousins teased me about this position, but I was a proper Metenem, even if I was half-Suese, and I was not going to abandon the correct way of sitting just because my mother's relations had not the advantage of a proper education.

"This was the ghost of a woman who had been killed on the road. In that time it was illegal to carry silk anywhere in Suo unless you went by the Tax Road, but this woman had many hungry babies and she could not leave them alone for long. So she took the contraband road and asked old mother tree if she would bend down her branches and make sure that the Bandit-King's men did not see her. But old mother tree was sleepy in the sun, and she forgot to shelter the woman. Because of this, the brigands found her and they were very cruel, and she died on account of their cruelty."

I couldn't contain myself, "What did death look like?"

Grandma Bo looked at me oddly. "Well, death from the outside looks very unpleasant, but with my first husband, when they laid his body out, he looked quite cheerful. So I don't imagine that death is so terrible as we sometimes suppose."

I was relieved. Grandma Bo knew of every monster in all the bestiaries of the world, and even had the head of one hanging on the wall of her little cottage. If she did not know about the eel, there was no doubt that it did not exist.

⌂

"If you were old and I were old and all our bones were turned to gold, oh-ee! Oh-eee!"

This is what my Grandma Bo was singing as she rocked back and forth in the garden swing. She always assured me that the bones of old women turned to gold and that this was why they had to be treated with care, like precious things, and protected from grave-robbers. There had been a grave-robbery here, in my grandmother's town, when she was a little girl, and I don't believe she ever got over the excitement.

"When they bury you," I said, "I'm going to dig you up. Just to see if it's true."

"Thut, you are a naughty, wicked little boy," she replied with a toothless laugh. "I shall have to stay as a ghost and spank you with my stick. Such impiety!"

"I didn't mean to be impious," I explained. I was watching a parade of ants which were marching up and down a stick that I had tipped with honey. Their bead-like bodies were of great interest to an inquisitive boy like me. "My Masters say golden bones are a Suese superstition. I just wanted to know the truth."

⌂

I was ten years old when my Philosophy Master ordered me to follow him out of the city and up onto the Second Hill. The First Hill was the one where the Great Sages had met to form the laws and principles which are the foundation of Metenem society. The Second Hill is of a less dignified pedigree, and can thus be used by ten year old boys. It is one of those hills that has not quite made up its mind about being in a proper hill-shape, and looks something like a cleft tomato. Between its two slopes is the entrance to a cave. It is not known how deep into the earth this cave goes: it may go for miles and miles, or it may stop just short of the furthest that a lantern is able to burn.

Slung over my Master's back was a bag which had been continually squirming and squeaking all the way up the hill. Out of this he drew a human skull, which he placed on the ground before me, then a long, slender knife and a small rodent which in Ptemya is called a slug-rat, but in Suo is called an otiga, which means "no-ears." The Philosophy Master held the little creature down against a rock and slit its throat. That did not particularly startle me: I had seen Grandma Bo slaughter much larger animals, and that summer I had been considered old enough to hold the hind-legs of the goat that she was killing for Tinder-day dinner.

"You will die," my Philosophy Master said with great conviction.

"Why?" My heart jumped up into my throat. "What did I do wrong?"

I could see he thought it improper to laugh at me. "I will also die. I understand what this means.

You will die, but you do not understand. Think on it."

With that, he left me to contemplate the skull and the dead otiga.

I sat down and looked at the rodent. Metenem do not eat them, because they are considered dirty and uncouth. The Suese fry them in batter and make them into Smelly-Pie. I did not know yet how long I would be left there, or whether it was true that I would have to face death in the form of hunger, so I decided on a prudent course. I made a simple knife out of a shattered rock, as my grandfather had taught me, skinned the otiga, made a fire-drill, and constructed a tripod from which I suspended the skull, upside down, as a cooking pot.

While the meat simmerred I thought, one day, a hungry child might use my skull for a pot. I knocked on the side of my head a couple of times and affirmed that it was so. A little later I thought, If they do, I'm going to come back and haunt them. This put me in mortal terror. Immediately, I removed the skull from over the fire and ate my undercooked meat with great trepidation. Finally, I took the heart of the otiga and put it between the teeth of the skull.

This being being the best meat, I hoped that it would placate the ghost.

I slept very uneasily, troubled by dreams of seven-headed eels.

When my Master returned early in the morning, he found me awake, kneeling, and staring into the ashes of a fire filled with the bones of the otiga. The blackened human skull sat a little way off, with a small heart between its teeth and a cloud of flies buzzing around it.

Taking this for the product of my meditation, expressed in images, he nodded knowingly and profoundly and declared that he had no more to teach me. I was referred to a higher Master, and in this way became a Philosopher.

◬

I had completely forgotten about Grandma Bo's golden bones by the time that word came to my mother that the old woman had died. I was fifteen, firmly established in my Philosophic studies, and no longer believed in the tales of malicious older boys or ignorant Suese farmhands.

The journey from Ptemya to Suo took nearly a week. We rode in my father's magnificent private carriage, carved of the sacred heart-wood of towering mahoganies. I was dressed in a traditional set of seven Metenem garments which had taken my paternal grandmother three years to sew. My hair was long, tied back in the style of a student, and even my mother wore an elegantly embroidered Metenem dress and bent her head in gentle contemplation as we rode into Grandma Bo's town.

I was not prepared for the exuberance surrounding my Grandmother's death. Grief, back in Ptemya, is a quiet affair. Here all of my uncles, aunts, cousins, great-aunts, grandfathers, and various people whom I don't believe were related to me at all, were drinking cashew wine and singing mourning songs with great, undignified tears running down their faces. The death cloth which my grandmother had woven in the last years of her life was held aloft, and everyone marveled and praised the fingers of the recently deceased.

Children were everywhere, milling around underfoot or gathered around the woven casket, drawn by their natural curiosity about death. They pulled back a little as I approached. I must have appeared as some sort of legendary figure, dressed in such fine clothes, with my dark Metenem complexion, and the children looked at me with something like supernatural dread. I smiled at them and knelt respectfully at the casket-side, contemplating my dead Grandmother's face.

It was entirely unsatisfactory. The dead are obligated not to look at all as they have looked in life. The skin is supposed to sag from the crags of their bones, the stuffing placed inside their cheeks to "fill them out" ought to create the impression of puffiness and swelling rather than natural grace. The paint plastered over the features is meant to be too bright, too vivid, so that the overall result is a caricature, barely recognizable as the beloved. Then everyone can have the pleasure of repeating "She doesn't look at all like herself," and be reassured that life has really come to an end.

Grandma Bo displayed no such seemly deathliness. Her eyes had refused to entirely close, and she looked as though she was peering out from under the thin lashes. No one had had to fix up her smile, as she appeared to be laughing slyly at the great joke of her death. The lines and wrinkles of her face had settled themselves as though in sleep, and she retained enough of her natural rosiness that when the aunts arrived, with their ghoulish paints, they had been quite at a loss and had confined themselves to a touch of comic rouge on her cheek-bones. How am I supposed to grieve for you? I demanded, with you looking like that?

Very distinctly, and quite unfairly, I heard a voice say, "I have to keep an eye on you, to make sure that you don't go trying to steal my bones."

I looked around. It is a stupid instinct, when one knows perfectly well that the thing they have heard has no earthly source, but I, in my quest for Metenem wisdom, had grown quite astonishingly stupid.

I did not want to be caught talking to myself in my good suit, so I whispered as if mouthing prayers. "I'm too old for that. I know your bones aren't gold – that's just nonsense for children. You can go to your star without worrying about that."

"Pish-piddle," said Grandma Bo, "You know no such thing."

She did not, fortunately, say anything else. But I wanted to be able to unbutton the little flap of skin at her throat to look inside for a hint of gold. I felt very foolish.

⌂

The thought of Grandma Bo's skeleton shining like the sun in an ancient tomb continued to torment me after the women had finally finished admiring the death-cloth and placed it over of her too life-like corpse. Then we all drew up into a rag-tag funeral procession, clattering along with shakers, flutes, and makers of noise to reassure Grandma's spirit that there would be plenty of descendants left behind to people the earth.

The road to the place where Grandma Bo's ancestors had been cremated for generations wound like a tipsy scythe through bulwarks of dense jungle to the cavern of the dead. Grandma Bo's casket was placed in the middle, and its woven lid put on.

The moment that the women let go of the lid, it popped up off the casket. While they were going to replace it, I distinctly saw Grandma Bo's ghost, like a child sneaking out of the pantry, sit up and creep out over the edge. She gave me a very severe look not to tell on her, and then tip-toed through the crowd. As soon as she reached the lip of the cavern, she began to run, her old, blue-veined legs flying out behind her, and her feet bare.

Various relations chased after her to convince her to climb back into her casket and follow her ashes up to the stars. We found her sitting in her little cottage.

"Mother Bo," my father said, "all the stars were shining on the moment of your death." By this he meant that she could not deceive the heavens.

"I know that perfectly well," she replied. "I am not one of these stupid ghosts that does not know that it is dead."

"You ought to know well enough to go back to your casket then."

"Pish-piddle, N'Toem," she replied. "What do you Metenem know? I have to stay here. I have to tell my grandson a bed-time story, and that is still many years away. Now here is what I want you to do with my bones when you have burnt up my body: it is important that you hide them in a special place."

My father looked at me to say, "I can see that this is all your fault," but there was nothing to be done. My grandmother would not be moved.

⌂

For my seventeenth birthday, I was given a student. His name was Zhilu, and he was eleven years old; a spindly-limbed, fat-bellied boy with a boxer's tongue and the left-jab of a poet. The many years of psychological torture inflicted on me by my own Masters had left me well prepared for my role as teacher.

"Kneel," I instructed, demonstrating the perfect posture that years of practice had made natural.

He slouched down like a sunken bag of rice and looked up at me with blind terror. After half an hour of prodding him with a stick, he managed a rough approximation of a straight spine. "Now," I continued – but before I could give him his assignment, his bum slid off his heels to the left and his tongue was earnestly investigating a gap in his front teeth. "Sit still!" I ordered, calmly smacking his wayward rear-end with the stick. He started to snivel. "Go home," I told him, "You're a disgrace."

The next day his mother came with a large feather duster to intercede on behalf of her son. The form of her plea was to beat me about the head and accuse me of heartless disregard for a boy who had lost his father in infancy, and who had already been dismissed by four Philosophy Masters, all on account of Philosophy Masters being spoiled, lazy and ungrateful creatures who committed every sort of impiety and despised the wombs that gave them birth. It was then that I understood that my own Masters had maliciously assigned me this student in recompense for my sins, which included daydreaming during meditation, and a pernicious refusal to repent of being half-Suese.

As I could not prove myself incapable of the task set me, and as Zhilu's mother's duster stung like a nest of wasps, I was compelled to take him on.

⌂

Zhilu proved entirely incapable of learning proper Metenem habits, and I did not know how to teach him to do anything without relying on tricks and cheats learned from my Suese relatives. So I decided that I had better teach him to be Suese. I went to his mother and told her that I would bring Zhilu back in a month. She cried, and beat me with her broom, but I was resolute. What could she do? No one else was going to teach her disobedient son.

I went to my mother and said, "I'm going to see Grandma Bo."

Immediately, as though she had guessed this months ago, she dipped into one of the magic cupboards in the back of her tea-shop and produced two-weeks traveling supplies and a shoulder-basket full of the largely random gifts that Suese habitually heap upon one another. I was supposed to distribute these to various relatives.

We set out. For two days, we walked through the pleasant Metenem country-side, stopping frequently at the tea-shops to have some rice-rolls and a pot of properly brewed tea. Then we arrived at the edge of the rain forest. It was marked by a guard-post. "There are savages in the forest," the guards teased, "they will pour out leeches to drink your blood, and set you on fire, and grind your bones."

"Yes," I replied.

"I want to go home!" proclaimed Zhilu.

"Silence," I said. "We are going to Suo."

⌂

The heart of the great rain forest of Metenemya concealed many strange things. The ancient volcanic peaks were known, in ancient times, to be haunted by bright blue lights, and when the first settlers had come to these shores they had found the mass graves of an entirely unknown civilization. Zhilu, ignorant of these things, dragged his feet along behind me like a pair of leaded geese, and stared into the beautiful, emerald-encrusted woods with eyes full of terror. For lunch, I taught him how to catch a turtle, and showed him the Suese secret that these animals are born into their own oven. He ate hungrily while I consulted the sky to discover whether we had been making good time or not.

It was getting towards supper when we heard the sound of human voices in the distance. They were not speaking Metenem, but a strange, distorted dialect of Suese which I couldn't understand at all. Zhilu learned very quickly how to climb a tree.

From the upper foliage, we could see the men passing beneath us: pale, nearly naked, decorated with elaborate scars and tattoos, with sinister obsidian knives hanging from lapis-lazuli belts. My student's fingernails dug into the bark of the tree, and I could smell the pungent scent of his urine.

"You're a disgrace," I reminded him when the danger had passed, but I let him go off quietly to wash his things in a stream.

⌂

The next day, around the middle of the afternoon, we reached the bridge across the Tiger River. Zhilu, terrified that it was overlooked by savage archers, refused to cross. I tried to carry him, but he kicked like a mule until I dropped him on the ground.

"All right," I said. "We'll go down-river and swim."

16

I solemnly commanded absolute silence as we picked our way through the dense undergrowth. At last we found a promising place, where the mud-flats extended into the stream, and there was little current. I was just about to step out of hiding, when I saw a conspicuously hungry looking log peering out of the shadows. I looked at the crocodile, which didn't seem to have noticed me, assessed the fact that it was about twice my size, and took a moment to meditate on the frenzied flapping of herons entrapped in its brothers' teeth. I had just started to edge back from the river bank when Zhilu, noticing the creature, cried, "Master! Look out!"

The hungry eyes flashed towards him, and with alarming speed the lizard emerged from the water. As my student could not be reasonably relied on to successfully run for his life, I grabbed a pointy stick and jabbed the monster in the breast, hoping to dissuade it from its dinner. In reply, it swung its head around and sunk its teeth into my lower leg. After the first shock of mind-blackening pain, my body saw fit to conceal from me the status of my limb until the threat had passed, and I found myself possessed of a remarkable clarity of thought.

For some time, we argued about who was the rightful possessor of my calf, the main thrust of my argument being directed towards its eye, which I eventually succeeded in puncturing. The crocodile found this line of reasoning sufficiently convincing to concede that it was entitled to only a small portion of my leg. It slunk off into the river to nurse its injury.

Zhilu was standing higher up on the river bank, looking like a petrified ground-weevil. "Get down here and pull me away from the river!" I growled.

Zhilu dragged me into the bushes with all the delicacy of a leopard dragging a dead gazelle. By the time that we were properly hidden, I was a useless mass of flesh that occasionally gibbered.

⌂

When I regained consciousness, it was getting dark. Zhilu was looking at me with eyes that glowed a terrified green in the darkness. "You're going to die," he whispered helpfully, looking as though this was a greater imposition on him than on me. I could see his point. If I died he would probably die too, but first there would be a great deal of wandering around lost in the jungle, wondering whether he was going to be dismembered by leopards, or ensnared by tree spiders, or fall into a bottomless ravine, or be devoured by giant slugs. All I had to worry about was whether I would die quickly of blood loss, or slowly of gangrene. "I tried to bandage your wounds," he said. I looked down. My shirt was a blood-soaked rumple loosely gathered around my leg. Flies were starting to assemble.

"I can see that. Take it off, and listen closely. This is what you must do to prevent infection."

By the time that he had come back with a handful of blood-worms dug up from the wet soil and had settled them on the edges of the tear to suck up any pestilence, it was pitch-black. The moon was a lazy scythe sweeping through the stars and humming to herself as she scoured the ground for something to snack on in the wee hours. "This is what you are going to do," I said, and sent him off down-river. My best chance was for him to go get help in Tiger's Foot.

He headed off like a herd of wildebeests stampeding drunkenly through the bush. For half an hour I waited, looking up at the sky. My name-star was meandering slowly across the horizon to the south. I could see all of my ancestors gathering to scold me for having imagined that I could teach a failed Metenem to be a Suese jungle-child.

⌂

"Grandma Bo?"

"Yes, Thut?"

"Tell me a story. About death. He's here, sneaking around in the ferns. He's trying to be quiet, but I can't hear anything except his breathing."

"Go to sleep. He's not grown very big yet. He will have to get much stronger if he's going to carry you off."

"I'm afraid of him," I said, matter-of-fact.

"Of a little baby death like that? He's hardly just a pup. You had better eat some of your mother's baking. He will grow quickly if you don't eat."

"I feel sick."

"In that case, you had better just sleep. Close your eyes and I'll sing you a lullaby."

I closed my eyes. I could feel the bloodworms sucking at the edges of my wound, and Grandma Bo's hand stroking my forehead. It was surprisingly warm for the hand of a ghost. She sang in her croakedy old woman's voice, an old song that distracted me from the sound of death growing stronger in the bushes.

⌂

Morning arose, sly and spiteful, taunting me with threats of rain and mosquitoes. My bandage was soaked through with something yellow and unpleasant smelling. I changed it slowly, trying not look at the churned up mass of dead white flesh swimming in the remains of my calf.

I had more important worries. Zhilu had left me with few supplies, no firewood, and only a few drops of water. This had a very serious implication: no tea. I had a beautiful tin of richly aged leaves, and no means of turning of them into the life-giving brew whose advantages the Sages have written so eloquently about ever since the discovery of that thaumaturgic leaf.

The river seemed impossibly far away, and there was every risk that it was infested with a tribe of vengeful crocodiles bent on repaying the loss of their brothers' eye. Still, it was possibly worth it.

I was considering the problem, and experimenting with various odd means of locomotion, when I heard death growling in the brush behind me. No. Not death. I could see her now, a wild dog, no doubt scavenging to feed her mongrel brood. She looked at my leg as if to say, "Are you done with that yet?" and sniffed around the pile of abandoned bandages.

I took a hunting knife out of my pack and looked over the top of the blade at the dog. "Dog," I said, "do you know the difference between you and I?"

If she did, she wasn't saying.

"The difference is that I can ponder the difference. I can put the question to you. You cannot put it to me."

"Maybe I could," her look said. "but should I bother?"

"Indeed. It doesn't seem a great advantage." I shifted my line of argument. "The difference is, I have a knife. It is long, and it is sharp."

She smiled and bent back her head. "I," she said with a sinister howl, "have a pack."

It was difficult to refute. One hunting dog I could probably beat off. Six? Eight? The mystery of movement suddenly opened to me, as in a moment of illumination: I could walk, and I could even climb trees. I simply had to get over my unwillingness to suffer excruciating pain.

Sitting in the branches of the nearest tree, I watched as six wild dogs assembled to conduct an investigation of my pack. They were very thorough: whatever they could not eat, they scattered. That was reasonable enough. They hoped that by tomorrow I would be prey. Best to weaken me first.

When they had finished a light snack of sundried squid and eel jerky, they sauntered off into the forest on the trail of some other scent.

Very slowly, I descended. The last crumbs of my breakfast were being carried away by ants. I couldn't afford to stay and wait for Zhilu. There was only one road that ran through the jungle, and if I followed it in the same direction that he had gone, I would be sure to meet my rescuers part-way. I made myself a crutch, and abandoned everything else, except for my knife, my canteen, my flint, and my tea. I headed off towards the bridge.

⌂

Death did not stay behind to root around in my scattered possessions. Behind me in the trees, I could hear him stalking: now a sleek leopard with a black coat, now a woman with a cap of raven's feathers, now a star that rose red on the horizon, threatening night.

Darkness came stealthily, while I was absorbed in twilight contemplations, and I realized that I was utterly exhausted, starving, and very thirsty. The tinkling of a forest stream seduced me into that most dangerous of errors. I stopped moving. Immediately, I desired to become as those monks who so root themselves in silent meditations that moss and vines mistake them for a home, and they become, at a distance, indistinguishable from tree-stumps or boulders in the green.

I drank, entertaining this glorious fantasy, and when I looked up I saw death sitting across from me on the opposite shore, crouching down on his haunches in a shadow.

He had grown.

⌂

When I woke the next morning I did a calculation. Even at his slowest pace, Zhilu would reach Tiger's Foot in two days. One was already behind me. A man on horse could cover the distance in a few hours. So I had one day and one night ahead of me, at most. "Come on," I told my leg. It rebelled. I pulled off the blood worms, washed the wound in the stream and cut away the worst of the dead flesh. "The long absence of suffering is more dangerous than a foreigner's wares," I instructed. The leg considered this maxim with a sour expression, but obeyed.

I walked slowly, leaning heavily on my make-shift crutch, looking out for anything that might be eaten. Mangoes were out of season, and the figs were too high in the trees for me to reach. At mid-day, I found a moldy guava covered in grubs. I lit a fire, and had crispy roast grubs for lunch. I told myself that they tasted like shrimp.

As I walked towards night, a figure walked next to me. Sometimes it looked like Grandma Bo, sometimes like death. "Grandma," I said once when it looked benign. As it turned a cadaverous face towards me, I did not confess that I was hungry.

⌂

"Grandma Bo?" I had collapsed, with very little dignity, on the side of the road. Dignity, or at least the Metenem conception thereof, had, however, lost its meaning. I didn't care that I had torn my pants down to little more than a loincloth, nor that I had smeared my face with pine resin to keep away the biting bugs.

"Yes Thut?"

"Death is not little anymore."

"No. He has grown. I can hear him sharpening his knife down by the river, but don't allow that to frighten you. It is an old trick of his, to make you despair. You had better eat."

"I don't have anything."

"You forgot about the nut-bar in your pocket."

I fished about in my jacket. There, wrapped in rice-paper bearing my mother's orchid seal, was a bar of cashews with honey and dried cherries. Grandma Bo was lying. I had not forgotten it; it had never been there. She had put it in my jacket, just as she used to hide candies in our pockets and pretend not to know where they had come from. I ate ravenously.

◊

I had been walking for nearly three full days. My leg was a useless weight of dead flesh dangling from my hip. Towards evening, death put a rock in my path when I was too exhausted to notice it. I tripped. The air flooded from my lungs, and the ghost of my leg briefly came back to haunt me.

Death put on his woman's face, and knelt beside me on the road. "You ought to know," she said, "all things living are my children. Do you not recall my face at the moment of your birth?"

"I was born in Suo. All my relations were there to crowd you out."

"I was there. I will be there until the day when you return to my womb. Why should it not be today? There is no evil in it."

"I am tired," I admitted.

"Yes."

"And I hurt."

"A great deal."

"And I'm very hungry."

"Never again," she promised.

"Unfortunately, I am half-Suese. And I haven't any children to make noise at my funeral." I turned my face and closed my eyes. "Go away."

She didn't. She sat there beside me and toyed with my hair while the flies landed to make their nests inside my mouth.

⌂

When morning came, Death was gone. It was strangely easy to rise and to walk. Foolishly, thinking that I had come through the worst, I picked up my stick, bullied my body into shape, and set out. I even

27

managed to whistle an old Suese lullaby to myself as I hobbled jauntily along the path.

Not far ahead, Zhilu was sitting at the side of a river. The river had been swollen by distant rains, and it had become so large that it had swallowed up its banks and was running treacherously over the top of the bridge, its waves like playful fish leaping and jumping and hoping to catch the feet of anyone who tried to cross.

Near the river-bank, Death emerged from the bushes in the guise of a child. His hair was black, and his eyes were deep and hungry, and all of his bones were clearly visible through his back. But my student did not see his back, and did not know enough to tell death from a friend.

Death sat down beside Zhilu and noticed that he was crying. "What's wrong?"

"I'm hungry," Zhilu admitted. "And I hurt my ankle trying to cross the bridge. I nearly fell off and drowned. And I've never had a father. And my Philosophy Master is very mean and always calls me a disgrace."

"Come with me," death said sympathetically. "At my house, no one ever gets hungry."

Zhilu looked down at his slightly swollen ankle, and at the empty pack of supplies which he had gobbled up in four days. He was about to agree when he heard the sound of someone shuffling along on the road.

"Disgrace!"

He made a sour face.

"There is a snake behind you, and it is going to kill you."

Zhilu was of one of those lower orders of prey which upon realizing a danger freezes up in the hopes that predators will be deceived by lack of motion. He made a small, undignified squeal. Death smiled as the snake slithered an inch closer to my student. As I could not think how I was going to explain to Zhilu's mother that her darling boy had died of cowardice and stupidity on the road to Suo, I forced myself to run and attempted to catch the snake around its milk-white throat.

I missed. I knew this by the feeling of sharp fangs embedding themselves in the back of my hand, and in the fire that started to spread through my arm. "Give me a knife," I shouted at Zhilu, and when he was not quick enough I tore the back of my hand open with my teeth and started to suck out the poisoned blood. The snake stayed nearby for several moments, swaying back and forth like a candle flame. I spit a mouthful of venomed blood at her, and she slithered away.

"Master?" all seven of Zhilu's heads said in pale-faced alarm. Behind him the trees of the jungle were pulling themselves up like ships from their moorings, and the sky was turning itself around like a child spinning a globe. I was pulled along into the wake of these upheavals, and hadn't time to construct a wise and pedagogic answer before I was whisked from the world.

⌂

At his gates, death waded through dark water in the form of a seven-headed eel. "Childhood spook," I accused him.

He opened all of his mouths, showing off his long, crystalline teeth. I was far too tired to be frightened by such phantasmagoria, and seated myself quietly on a rock. Far out in every direction I could see the world as a sea; towns and cities, forests and mountains, rocking back and forth slowly to the rising and ebbing tide of death and life. Above, the stars were firm and undisturbed, and there were pathways winding up to them beyond the gate.

Death, seeing that I intended to be patient, settled in the form of a wizened old man bending over his toll-booth at the side of the road. On his coins were the skulls of men. "Surrender," he suggested.

"What are your terms?"

"I'm offering rest. You are very much in pain, I think."

"Yes."

"You are only afraid to follow me, because you do not know where I will take you. But why should you assume I mean you ill?"

"Because flies gather."

"There are no flies here."

It was true. The flies were down below, forming clouds and citadels on the slopes of the waving earth. They were gathering around my skull, and forming alliances with centipedes to conquer the inner reaches of my brain. "No. There are no flies here."

"The gate is wide, and it is open, and the cost I exact is very small."

"Yes. But what is the cost of the other path?"

"You cannot pay it."

"My Grandma Bo," I offered, "has golden bones, which are buried in a secret place where you would never be able to find them. I know where they are."

Death contemplated this for a moment, going carefully over his ledgers and discovering that what I said was true.

"You will give them to me?"

I nodded.

The deal was struck.

⌂

I apologized to Zhilu, as soon as I awoke, for having been so negligent as to allow him to go on ahead of me as though he had already learned what was required to survive. "Now," I said, "we will have a lesson. You will learn the ancient art of carrying a Philosophy Master on your shoulders across a swollen river when the bridge is submerged." After this, I taught him the very valuable lesson of how to make a stretcher out of a jacket and two poles, and how to hitch it to his back and pull without complaining. When we arrived in Tiger's Foot, I felt that he had shown adequate improvement and was entitled to a rest. At the tea-shop, I introduced him to the pleasures of smelly-pie, and the abominable practice of adulterating one's tea with Suese hooch.

I allowed him to sleep for a couple of hours, curled up in a pile of hay, while a Suese madman poured noxious potions into my leg and chanted a healing rhyme and hammered the teeth of a grass snake into the sound flesh just above the injury. He explained that the spirit of the animal would frighten off the night-wind when she came to lay her evil brood in my wound.

In the yard of the tea-shop was a cart with a broken wheel. I secured permission to borrow it, on the condition that I would return it with the wheel wrighted in two weeks time. It bumped and jostled my leg painfully, but I was willing to endure such suffering for the sake of Zhilu's training. "Straighten your back," I called out to him as he struggled, puffing, at the traces. "If you pull with improper posture, you will break."

⌂

Four days later, we arrived at my Grandmother's town. Since Suese relations possess an extra sense that tells them when visitors are coming, there were about seven hundred and fifty cousins, aunts, grandfathers, nieces, nephews, and miscellaneous folks waiting on the road when we arrived. Immediately, half of the women untied my student from the harness, and carried him off to spoil him with treats. The other half fussed like a clutch of hens over my leg, and contradicted each other over remedies and medicines. When at last I escaped from their ministrations, I discovered Zhilu sitting beside a fire, with all of my cousins gathered around to make fun of him for his perfect Metenem posture. I slumped down beside him like a bag of rice. "We are in Suo," I explained.

After we had eaten a meal of deep-fried otiga and plum-wine, I asked if Grandma Bo's cottage was still as it had been. "Oh yes," my relations assured me. "But you would not want to sleep there tonight. Her ghost must be very angry, I think. For, I tell you with my own tongue, there was a grave-robbery in our village only one week past, and her secret bones have been carried off!"

I said that I should like to stay there anyway.

⌂

That night, while Zhilu slept peacefully, in spite of his terror of ghosts, I crept out of bed and over to the fireplace. Grandma Bo was sitting by the fireside, in her old chair, looking at an empty cup and dreaming of milky tea.

"I'm sorry," I said. "About your golden bones."

"Pish-piddle," she replied. "What on earth do you imagine I hid them for?"

The Exhibition

•••••

They were laid out on a pallet of ice dragged down from the mountains, their drugged forms folded against each other like a cut of fresh raw meat. The gallery had opened less than hour ago, but the exhibits had been arranged early enough to allow the flesh to grow white from the frostbite, and the lips on their down-turned faces to darken to blue. The murky green and grey light, filtered through the arching stained glass ceiling, added to the impression of inhumanity and made the freezing bodies on the table look as though they were already rotten even though they were not yet dead.

Across an aisle cluttered with murmuring critics, a glassy eyed form was laid like a half-filleted fish, the skin of his chest stretched back to reveal God's handiwork. His lungs inflated and exhaled to a slow tempo, pumping the icy blood slowly through the carefully exposed veins. Beside him, another had been shaved of all hair, his legs stretched and broken at the hip-socket, then tucked in underneath his body. It was impossible to tell whether the thick, slightly rusted iron spit that slid between those disjointed legs and emerged at the base of his neck actually ran through his entire body, or whether it was only an illusion – in either case it had been carefully done, and though a heavy dose of sedatives kept him from screaming and disturbing the visitors, it was clear that he was still alive.

This was the first exhibition that Garnet had braved in over a century. In those days the fashion had been deliberate deformity; men made with the faces of beasts, or misshapen into the likeness of a turning screw. The art of it had been to make the most severe possible departure from the human form, without creating something too monstrous to be viable; apparently, things had grown worse in a hundred and fifty years.

"Give us a blessing, little mother." The man standing next to Garnet clearly fancied himself a critic of the arts. He was dressed in the new-style – layers of expensive cloth and furs draped so that they loudly proclaimed the wealth of one who could afford natural fabrics, while doing nothing to clothe or obscure the body of the wearer. His laugh was as joyless and acerbic as bubbling vinegar.

"That one only blesses monsters," his companion, who was neither male nor female, sipped its wine and ran its fingers along the surface of the blood-drenched ice.

"But aren't we all monsters, darling? After all, aren't we all monsters?"

Garnet did not respond to this exchange. Her legs were weak and she clung to the jeweled grip of an expensive wooden cane. It was the one extravagance that she still allowed herself – that cane, and a thin robe of real organic fabric from beyond the wasteland. Her body was too thin to support a metal shirt, and even when she had been young, and her clay damp and supple, her legs had not been thick enough to hold her up unaided. It had been a matter of economy: clay was required to make a body, and clay was the only currency of any real value. Now, as the centuries passed, and her clay started to dry and crumble, it was becoming difficult to walk, even with these luxuries.

The people on display were different. They had been shipped in from a distant battlefield, and their bodies were made not of clay, but of flesh. They weren't capable of withstanding the temperature of their icy bed, and by the time the gallery closed tonight they would be dead. The exhibit would go on. Fresh ice would be loaded into the rail-cars, and fresh prisoners brought from the war, and in the morning the artist would arrive to rearrange his masterpieces before the gallery opened.

⌂

When she could no longer bear to stand vigil over the dying, Garnet retreated to one of the old wings of the gallery. In a room filled with the crumbling blocks of an ancient fresco she collapsed in weariness. The stones were damp, and the water dripped from them like pus from a wound, but nothing -- not a spot of moss or mildew -- had grown over the painted images. They were scenes from a life lost millenia ago, the icons of a saint who Garnet, for all her centuries, had never known. Little remained of the painting, which had once stood as tall as a cathedral. It had taken ten years to paint it: the last act of hope committed by a suicide. "You were too weak for this world," Garnet told the painter. "And too much of a coward." She meant, Why have you left me alone with this inheritance of suffering?

The stones did not answer. She lowered her head, and allowed exhaustion with the present to consume her. In the sleepless rest of her kind, she slipped into a memory as vivid as a dream.

⌂

From the moment that he stepped into the council chamber, defeat had been carved out of the too-thin planes of his face. He had once been a tower of wealth and glory. His body, crafted of immortal clay seized from the foundation of the world, had been a monument to the grandeur of creation. A single scraping from his back might have mortgaged an ordinary man. Now his body had been pillaged. Layers of clay painstakingly scraped away from his back, his legs, his chest, his cheeks hollowed out, his limbs sliced off and reattached so that the valuable connecting material could be excised. The priestly robes that he had once filled like a demi-god hung limply from his awkward frame, and he walked like a poltergeist held together by pain.

They had been the architects of revolution -- but the gaping teeth of the torture chambers did not yawn for them. The accused were lined up across the back of the council chamber, their arms twisted and held in bolted manacles, their faces haggard with the realization that they were being abandoned to suffer the sentence for High Treason. Neither Garnet nor the painter could bear to look towards their one-time allies. Both knew, from the way in which they could not meet each others eyes, that their treachery had been mutual.

⌂

Garnet wrenched herself back to consciousness, before she had to relive the rest. This was the risk of memory: that the traitor psyche would pull you into something more painful than the present. "We wanted so much to save our own lives," she told the stones bitterly. "We ended up sacrificing a civilization."

The stones did not answer. They had died long ago, unable to bear the weight of betrayal.

⌂

She took the long way back to the exhibit, down a roadway paved in dull gemstones, curving through a forest of lusterless glass and metal trees. The heavy sky leaned menacingly on the world, threatening a rain that it had not delivered for centuries. It was this way wherever her people settled -- they brought the wasteland with them, in their hearts, and in their bodies; in the turning of their machines in the fertile soil; in the roots of their civilization which twisted into the ground like an iron screw into a living body.

The foil and crystal garden was supposed to give the impression of created beauty, just as the stained glass walls were supposed to filter the eternal drabness into something that resembled colour. Even from here, though, she could see the world around her as it really was. The serpentine curlings of the rails as they ran across the damp and inorganic desert. The huge bodies of the 'monsters' running the train-cars -- men of pitch and gravel, cast in moulds instead of sculpted, crudely fashioned to be cheap and useful; a race of disposable slaves, so primitive and inarticulate that it was easy to imagine them devoid of souls. They called Garnet their mother, and she was so in a double sense. She recalled, with regret but no longer with pain, that she had been the first to make such creatures. Hers had been of clay, and not of lesser materials, but still deliberately deformed, robbed of intelligence, given life so they could serve as tools. Human conveniences.

The second sense was new. A result of the painter's stamp on her life, before he had taken his own: he had bequeathed to her his priestly robes, the

43

right to bless, and the obligation to serve even the lowest and most inhuman of their kind. Garnet managed a very thin smile, which cracked the drying corners of her mouth. Several flakes of valuable clay, too dried out to be of further use, flaked off and settled in the breezeless twilight. From the pocket of her robes, she drew out a small, dried up plum. Once she had walked through a real orchard, where the fruit that swung from the branches was full of juice and life. Here, even this was a luxury. She lifted it to her lips, and bit off the tiniest of all possible fragments. The flavour was intensely delicious, a feverish wine, and she wanted to devour it with all the decadence that she had once enjoyed before she had traded power for an ideal, and an ideal for cowardice.

"You are not allowed here," a voice thudded; it was a voice of mud and silt. The man who spoke was one of the highest grades of monster. She could see the pebbles and dust moulded into his gravelly hands, but there was red there too -- real clay.

"Why is that?" she asked.

"You are not allowed here."

A sense of disappointment settled in her clay lungs. She had hoped that there was enough of the

44

currency of life in his body that he was capable of speech, but most likely his throat had been designed to utter only these sounds, his mind imprinted with a single series of words, and a command to show him when to use them. Speech, to him, was function, not communication. There were means by which the mangled and the mutilated learned to express themselves to one another. Signals of body, and of hand. But there were a thousand dialects, and Garnet would not have known his, even if he had tried to sign to her.

Speaking the only universal tongue, she held out the dried plum. The man stared at it dumbly as the minutes stretched, and then finally seized it between rough fingers and shoved it into the devouring gorge of his throat. A flicker of pleasure registered on the surface of his inexpressive form, so slight that only one as well versed as she in the art of reading bodies could have noticed it. She had learned that beneath these tiny signals lay a wealth of gratitude, inaccessible, but deeper than anything discoverable in the most finely crafted features of the rich. This was probably the only food-grade organic material he would ever consume in his life.

He swallowed and adjusted his stance. "You are not allowed here," he said. She nodded wearily and turned back towards the main gallery.

⌂

The exhibit had now been on for nearly three hours. Its novelty had started to wear off. Within a week the bodies freezing to death on the table would be considered a hackneyed joke. Another artist would invent an even more outlandish degradation. The corpses would be ground up into a paste with dirt and stone, and fed to the monsters. Nothing would be wasted. It was all such a waste.

There was nothing now, that she could do about it. Her chance to redeem the world had passed by centuries ago. She had given it up for a handful of dust. Nothing remained to her except a little known office, in a faith that had died with the suicide of its founder.

Clinging to her oaken cane, she walked towards the exhibition. The leg of one of the bodies had begun to twitch, seized by involuntary spasms. Another had already choked to death on his own tongue. She did not close her eyes, because this was the world that she had chosen, and she had to see it for what it was.

She extended one hand. Her skin was old and crackled, her voice as dry as burning paper. There was only one power that remained to her. In honour of their humanity, and in memorial of her own, she bowed towards the frozen men, and intoned the benediction for the dying.

THE IDOL'S GILDED EYE

· · · · ·

The little ship huddled on the waters at the foot of the silver cliffs, with a crew of refugees hiding in her womb, and the mouth of a river opening in front of her. Cast off from her bow, a wooden Water-Spider carried a party of explorers up the river, under a thick canopy of sharp-toothed palms and trailing mosses. Supposedly, they were going to find out if the land was "good to build a city." They all knew that even if it was infested with flying snakes and poisonous dragons, they were going to have to bring the families ashore. But all these civilized people liked to pretend they had a choice, even when nature had them bound up in her loom.

Litta held an oar and hummed a song from her own land, full of rhythm and deep sounds that came out of your gut and reminded you that your body was a part of your humanity, and of your past.

"Please," said the Narananti captain, "if you could be quiet." He was studying the jungle like an unskilled hunter searching for a war-pig.

"You have it in your breast, still," she said. "All that wall. You didn't leave it behind there on that shore. You didn't leave all those crook-necked old ladies with their dry mouths and their scoldings. You didn't leave nothing of it behind you. It's still here. Now I'm going to sing my song, and you're going to listen until a little of the jungle comes in to take that wall apart."

"We are here," he said calmly, "to find a good piece of land and found a city. Not to revert to savagery and chase ghosts through the woods."

"Then your city is going to be the same as the one you left. In a generation, your son is going to run away from its walls. Tell me, wall-builder, what kind of land you think he's going to run to?"

"I'm never going to have a son." The words dropped from Nidyom's lips like a stone into the water. "My wife would not come with me. She knew that men were losing their posts at the universities. That we were being sent to the fields and mines to work like beasts of burden. She had heard the rumors of castrations as 'a remedy for aggression.' She knew, though she denied it, that they were also a remedy for protest. But do you know what she said? My faithful wife? She said, 'You have been blessed with the work of the mind. Now be blessed with the work of the hands.' And when I insisted, she said, 'If you must, then you may take the knife in protest. I will go with you to the place of dying.' She said it as though it would be her martyrdom, to stand by and watch me die in a worthless gesture. But she would not leave the city with me."

"Then you don't have a wife. There are plenty of women on ship. You find yourself a good one this time."

"I will never have news of her death. She is still my wife, and we do not take more than one."

⌂

They landed around noon-time, on a little island of silt at a fork where two rivers joined into one. Litta named the place 'A good place for landing, where noon-time is evening' -- Tikapotaka-watawa-go. Nidyom named it Myetoa: 'where two rivers meet.' They didn't bother to fight about the name.

Eyes peered down from the trees above, and a thick sludge of bright, almost glowing algae had started to collect around the edge of the Spider. The air was thick with the smell of a mystery. Litta got out onto the slender tongue of silt that was sticking out into the water. She took a long knife from her pack and chopped a hole in the greenery at the edge of the river. There were places in the world where all the trees stood sentinel by the waterside, and if you could get into the interior it was possible to move freely. This was not the case here. The entire land seemed to be one vast, impenetrable mess of vines and surly, cankerous aloes. "We have to go further on," said Litta, and changed the name in her head to 'Full of evil plants with bad manners.'

Nidyom shook his head. "This is the best that we have come to in half a day's travel. We need to be able to make it back to the ship by evening. We're going to have clear a space as well as we can."

"What do you know about jungle?" Litta-Po demanded. "You don't want to work fields. In my land, we don't even know fields. We know gardens, and we know beasts. You go into combat everyday with the buffalo and the war-pig. Maybe you find you lose an eye. This is the kind of land you're coming to.

You think you're going to build a un-i-vers-i-ty in this?"

"I don't object to work. I object to slavery. We're stopping here."

"Kookti, soft-arms. You don't know about work. Well," she handed him the knife. "I guess you better start to learn."

⌂

"People!" Nidyom announced. His hands were blistered and cut up by the jungle, but his face was full of joy beneath the sweat. "Look at this!" He was kneeling beside a piece of jungle floor – the only piece that was not completely strangled with vegetation. Litta-Po walked over to where he was squatting.

She looked at Nidyom as though he were mad. "I don't see no one."

"Look!" he was pointing down at the ground. Litta-Po looked very closely. There were many different little stones laid up one against another. It was a road, like the roads that ran into the Naranantia, but all thrown up and usurped by the trees.

"Been a long time, now, since anyone walked down this," she said.

53

Nidyom didn't seem to notice. He took out his knife and began to slice away at the fronds that choked this relic of civilization.

"Don't we need to go back and get people from the ship? We clear all this space, make it so that the children have a little place they can put their blankets down, and now you going to go walking down some old donkey-path looking for people who no one's ever seen? Probably this path's been made by demons. If there were people in this part of the world, someone would have known about them."

"There is a road here. That means that there have been people. Go back to the ship with the others and tell them that they can come and set up camp. I'm going to go on ahead."

Litta-Po went back and told the others to go back to ship and bring everyone down the river to the camp-site. It was not much of a camp-site, she thought, but all that chopped down greenery would make a good bed. She only hoped that the trees in this jungle had benevolent spirits. Thinking about that road, all choked up, and the people who no one had ever met, she didn't think so. For a long time, now, people had seen the lights glowing over this land. There were watchers here of unusual power.

They lurked in the darkness, and they closed off roads, and they devoured the memory of a civilization. No. Litta-Po did not like the fact that the sea had chosen this place for them. She did not like the look of all the newly dead trees lying with their sap spilling into the soil. This was a place that didn't like people. Still, the ship was in no shape for going anywhere else. If they were going to be devoured, it was better than starving slow.

It didn't take her very long to catch up with the Narananti man. He didn't say anything to her when she joined him going down the broken road. They were silent together, working to cut a way down the path. It was hot even in the shade: a thick, sticky hot that made your clothes feel like an old fish skin draped across your shoulders.

Litta wished that she had never come here. It had seemed like a good idea at the time. When the ship of Narananti refugees had stopped on the shore near her village, looking for supplies, the old men of her tribe had said, "These are foolish soft-arms. They will need someone to teach them of the world. You go, and make sure that you keep the spirits of the wild from creeping into their bone. And keep

55

them from carrying the spirit of the dragon-city into the wild." This had seemed like sound counsel at the time. Now, Litta did not know how she was going to do anything to protect them.

The road stretched a long way before they came to the place where it crossed the river. There it ended in a high bridge built on pedestals of white stone which had been taken over by mildew. Once, it had risen like a titan astride the water, nearly twice Litta-Po's height. Now, it had all been thrown down, and the big, white blocks trailed green sea-weed hair into the flow of the stream. The river was not peaceful here. It was angry about the broken bridge. It gnashed at it with foaming lips. Nidyom climbed up onto the nearest of the toppled stones and began to pick his way across. It was not easy to walk: the stones were slippery, and in some places there were gaps that would have to be jumped. Litta handed the Narananti a stick so that he would be in less danger of falling in.

⌂

It was almost evening, and the jungle had opened up enough to let the eyes of the sky peer down over their heads. Litta kept a watch out to see if the lights would start to move over their heads. She realized that she should not have followed Nidyom down this path laid by demons. She should have stayed behind at the camp, and woven ghost-scarers to hang in the trees and protect the colonists.

Nidyom pushed aside a veil of leaves, then stopped, staring, with a sharply indrawn breath. Litta-Po crept up behind him and peered over his shoulder. There, draped in green, with little springs jumping over it like evil sprites, was a city built into the side of a ravine. The rock was steep and full of crevices where the snakes would go to sleep. It was covered with trees whose roots covered the mouths of doorways, and tore holes in long abandoned walls. Monstrous statues leered out from the shadows, crowned with mosses of purple and blue, their hideous eyes gaping from under veils of vines, their fattened tongues protruding from mouths filled with the weaver-spider nets.

Nidyom looked as though he had just discovered the promised land. Litta could see that whatever had happened here, it was a great evil. It still clung to the rocks. It clung to the stone in the center of the city, where an echo of blood that had long since washed away. Litta-Po knew that they should get away, but the spell of the city had worked its magic on Nidyom, and they would not be going unless she could break the enchantment.

"Wonderful!" he breathed. "What marvels!" He knelt beside a nest of broken pottery, picking up the detritus of dead men and studying it with the wild eyes of a scholar. "Look at these patterns. Look at this construction. Litta – this is not the home of savages. There was a civilization here."

Litta-Po looked at the patterns. They were very intricate, but not beautiful, full of sharp angles that led the eye into a tangle of lines from which there was no emerging. "A civilization, that I can see. But people? What good is a city to anyone if it is not able to keep its people? If it devours them whole and leaves only stone idols?"

"Ruins," Nidyom said sternly, "do not mean that a people has been devoured. Probably there is some reason that they had to leave."

Litta shook her head. In the shadows, she saw something crouching. A human form, dark, and perfectly motionless.

She pulled aside a curtain of dripping moss that hung down over the crevice where the figure huddled. It was a woman, too life-like to have been carved by the hands that made the monsters, bent

58

down to protect an infant clutched against her breast. Litta knew at once that this woman was real. What she did not know, was how a woman and child could be turned to stone.

⌂

Litta refused to spend the night in the city, but she could not convince Nidyom to come with her. He insisted that he was going to spend the night in one of the cavernous, empty tomb-houses where the people had been consumed many long-days before. He insisted that the woman crouching in the grotto had been killed in a volcanic eruption. He named the kind of rock that had embalmed her. He pointed to her wide open mouth, screaming as she rocked her baby. He described the great mountain that had spewed out fire like the blow-spout of a whale and said that the woman had been caught in its blowing and preserved. He said that she had died a long way away, and had been brought here, presumably as an object of worship. Nidyom did not know anything.

Litta went alone. It was dark, and there was nothing that she could bring to make a light. To ward off attack, she sang the protection song that she had learned as a girl. It was a strong song that stuck in the back of your throat and made you hoarse. You had to struggle against the pain in your gullet to make yourself keep singing. This was so that anything that might attack you would hear that your will was greater than theirs was. Especially if it was a ghost.

When she arrived at the place where the fallen stones bridged the river, it was almost too dark to see them, except as great, black hulks grinning toothily out of the water. Litta-Po could see that there was no way she was going to make it across before daylight dawned. She could hear creeping things in the forest behind her. A long howl, like a battle cry, rang from the trees, and a slithering army moved towards her in the dark. She sang louder, so that they would know that they did not frighten her. The song cut like a knife in her wind-pipe.

It was then that the lights began to fill the sky. They were strange lights, silver and green, tinged with golden yellow at their edges, with an eye of purple staring down from their midst. It was the eye of a demon larger than a mountain looking down at her from the starry heights. It was light enough to see by, but Litta was afraid. She did not want to take help from that monster in the sky. She did not want to go out into the open where it could see her.

The slithering increased behind her, and a sound like lips yawning. It was the beasts or the demon: one or the other was going to get her. Litta scrambled up onto the nearest of the rocks and began to pick her way across the river.

The light in the sky stretched, and the eye faded away in a splash of pink. Something had made it close its eye, just at the moment when it would have seen her. Litta thought of the old men of her village, casting their blessing-seeds out over the earth, and of the endless line of identity that stretched back amongst her people until the earliest days. She was an eddy in the current of that great stream, a branch of the tree that was her people. The sap still flowed from its source, way back at the beginning, and she was not severed from the blessings that were given far away. She pulled a couple of hairs out of her head and threw them into the river so that they would be carried home to remind her people of the part of themselves that had come to this strange land. Then she finished crossing the river and headed towards the camp.

⌂

There were almost fifty families who had come from the boat. They were stretched out on the broken green, with their torn blankets, and their bundles of treasures brought with them from Naranantia. The children were mostly asleep, though some of them were awake and crying in fear of the strange lights. The men were exhausted: it had fallen to them to enlarge the camp enough to allow everyone to sleep there tonight. Many of the women remained awake.

Litta had no friends amongst these women. They were all Narananti – they had come here with their husbands, and many of them were talking about how they should not have come. Litta had heard them on the boat over, constantly complaining about how much better it had been at home, and how much work was going to need doing in a new land. They had come to prevent their families from being broken. They held this over their husbands' heads.

Litta could see already that there was not going to be anything different here from Naranantia. Even though she found Nidyom insufferable, she felt a little sorry for him and his dreams. He thought of himself as their leader. He was really the little pet bush-pig that they trailed ahead of them in the jungle so that if there was something lurking in ambush, he would die to warn them.

Litta-Po didn't go over to where the women were sitting around their fire, spinning plans for the city that they were going to build. She squatted down on a pile of thick leaves and started weaving together the dolls of tough grasses that she would hang in the trees to keep their children safe.

⌂

When she arrived back at the abandoned city the next morning, Litta-Po could see immediately that all was not well. Nidyom was sitting on a bench of broken marble with a darkness in his eyes as though a spirit had come and possessed him in the night and stolen away the nugget of his soul. She walked up to him very slowly, waving a little piece of grass in front of her so that if the spirit was still there, it would not be able to come near her.

"Litta-Po." His voice was as broken as the ruins he was sitting in. He stood and a fractured smile broke across his lips. "Come with me," he said.

He led her up the side of the ravine, and down a road that had not grown over, as though the jungle was afraid to take possession of it. At the end of the road there was a pit, wide as a lake, full of bones. The skeletons had shed their flesh, and up through the rib-cages and the eyes of the skulls snaked long vines. Broken leaves of rust and brown draped like shawls over dust-white shoulders. The skeletons were of every age and size: even women with the bones of unborn children still bleaching in the hollow of their wombs.

"I think," said Nidyom, "that there are over a thousand here. And there's another like it over the next hill."

"This is a terrible war, you think?"

The Narananti shook his head. "Not war. No broken skulls. No shattered bones. No splinters where a blade had hit the rib-cage. These people did not die of violence."

Not human violence, thought Litta. "What are you thinking they died of?"

Nidyom shook his head. "They didn't bother with separate burials. They didn't take the time to fill the graves in. You can see," he said pointing to something gleaming deep within the piles of human remains, "their valuables thrown in underneath them. A treasure-trove, but it's never been robbed. Perhaps it was just their custom --"

"To leave the meat of their ancestors to rot in the sun? There are no such people."

"And it would bring disease. No. I think, Litta, that something terrible happened here. I don't think anyone survived."

It was the first time that Nidyom had shown a little intuition. He was right. Litta had known it yesterday, just looking at their homes. "It is because of the eye," she said, "that burns in the night. It looked down on them, and it did not like what it was seeing. I do not know what it saw, or whether it was evil that burnt them up, or evil that they were doing. It would be a good thing to know, because it tells us whether or not we can survive in this place."

"Probably a plague," said Nidyom. "A terrible plague that kills completely, and can't be contained."

"For a second," said Litta, "there was sense in your bones. Now you are speaking like a babbler. This was no plague. It was evil. You know that as well as I."

⌂

When they returned to the camp that afternoon, they found it in mourning. Three people had died in the night. Nobody knew why. They had shown no signs of sickness. They had not eaten the local fruits. It had not grown cold at night. But there, in the morning, they lay dead. Two men, one child.

Nidyom turned pale and didn't say anything. Litta-Po checked her ghost-scarers. They no longer hung in the trees. She found several clumps of burnt grasses scattered nearby. "Did you go burning these?' she demanded of the women.

"Your Mik-Mar superstitions do not bother us," they answered. "Now we need to go and mourn our dead."

Litta looked at the burnt up dolls. The ghosts of that pit were still living here. They had burned the dolls to show her they weren't afraid of her magic.

She sat down in the corner of the camp. The others were weaving a basket for the dead out of the leaves that they had cut down the day before. The Narananti women made no sound in their grieving. They painted their faces with charcoal-paste, and kept their mouths and eyes very still and did not say anything. The men sat in a circle around the perimeter of the camp and kept their eyes fixed on the ground so that they would not look on the silent rites of death. Only the children made a sound: two small boys weeping for their father. The dead were carried out to the river and set on it. The mourners made little fans out of palm fronds and waved a silent good-bye. When the woven caskets had sunk, the

Narananti threw the fans into the water. Then the families of the dead left the camp so that they could break their silence without anyone to see.

◭

There were two more deaths the next night. When they were discovered in the morning, Nidyom did not wait until the grieving rites were over before he left. Litta-Po followed him down the road, back to the city below the pit of bones. When she arrived, he was kneeling before the grotto of the dead woman, hunched over his own knife, with fear filling his eyes.

"You don't be stupid," she told him. "We don't need any other death to make this better."

"You don't understand," he said grimly. "I brought them to this place. I told them it was safe to get off the boat. It was at my insistence that we set sail from Naranantia. It was I who refused to stay on the islands because I was too proud to be a refugee in a colony of your people. I wanted to bear Naranantia with me. I wanted to make her anew, without the corruption in her heart. This was my dream. This is my failure."

"Is this what the death-side confession of a Narananti sounds like? It is just what I would have thought from a civilization of cowards. You are so proud, you people of the wall. You think that the whole world is going to fall to pieces if you don't hold it tight in your hands. You told me you left Naranantia instead of taking the knife. You said you weren't going to kill yourself in this stupid gesture. Now what do you think to accomplish with this foolishness? Get up, and we're going to find out how to stop these people being dead."

"A thousand bodies, Litta. A thousand in a single grave. They did not figure out how to stop the deaths."

"And they don't have the Mik-Mar people to stand among them and call up the strength of all the time since the world began. Probably, just like you, they kneel down and cry themselves out in despair. Now get up. We've got a great magic to work here. You aren't Mik-Mar, but you could be if you put the wall out of your heart and turn into a man. Now come and be my help."

Nidyom shook his head. He had not found a way to find his soul again. It was still stolen, hidden amongst the boxes of treasure at the bottom of the grave. He had looked too deeply, thought Litta, and not with enough hope. The knife went into his belly with a whimper. Litta did not paint her face black or weave him a coffin of silent leaves. She knelt over his body and sang a song of keening and pain – a song so deep in her gut that the Narananti must have heard it all the way back in the camp, and covered their faces for shame at hearing such grief.

⌂

There was not time to bury the body. She knew that it would begin to rot quickly in the heat. It was not fitting to leave him in this state. Yet it was essential that she begin her work immediately. He was a suicide. He had chosen this ignominious decay. Still, he had been Litta's only friend, and she did not like to leave it that way.

With the pain still clinging close to her bones, she went through the streets of the broken city, looking into the houses where termites ate away the remains of furnishings, and spiders the size of Litta's hand built massive webs across the ceilings. Somewhere, in all of this, there had to be a clue. It was the first thing necessary: to find out the truth. Only when the disease has been diagnosed does the singer know which song to sing to draw it out.

The houses were silent. Anything of value in them – anything that might have spoken of the people who had lived inside of them had been taken out.

It was only in the last of the houses, the one nearest to the graves, that she found something that might lead to knowledge. It was a stone door set in the furthest corner of the darkest room, blocked off by a pile of fur and tiny bones left behind by a nocturnal bird. Litta rubbed her fingers raw prying open the door. The little bones crunched like grain under a millstone. It opened on a passageway entirely consumed by darkness, with damp recesses that dully glinted back the tiny fragment of light that spilled in through the door.

Since it was impossible to see, Litta closed her eyes and edged forward. The ceiling was too low for walking; Litta crawled. Carapaces of starved-out beetles broke and shattered beneath her knees. Something tiny bit at her ankles in the dark: the needle-soft stinging of insects which might have been poisonous. A dizziness stirred in her veins.

At last the passage ended. A little light filtered in from above, but through a gruesome curtain. The gold and valuables that Nidyom had seen glinting underneath the bodies were spread out at the far end of a small chamber: the light came in

70

on a slant through a forest of bones. In the center of the chamber there was a small box. Litta approached it slowly and pried it open. It was made of stone. Dust circled it like incense, and a scattering of blue-gold beetles, small and round as peas, trickled out like a stream of living jewels. Inside were human skeletons, too tiny ever to have been born, their rib-cages split open by the savage intrusion of a knife. Litta-Po shuddered and held one of the tiny, egg-shell skulls in her hands. In the pits where its eyes ought to have been, she could see the mothers laid out on the floor, the noxious brew forced past their lips, labor brought on too early, and the children, too small to survive, speared on the sacrificial blade. The dark god to whom this had been offered was carved into the wall before her. Litta shook to the center of her gut. It was an image that she recognized: the dragoness, patron of Naranantia. She lifted the box with its precious remains, and removed it from the sight of the idol's gilded eyes.

⌂

She stood in the stream at midnight, when the dragon's bright eye was opening over the world and seeking human souls to devour. In her hands she held the children who had never breathed. She had

71

wrapped them each in a large, flat leaf, and tied each around with a thin braid of her hair so that when she set them to float on the river, and they flowed out to the ocean from which all life arose, their spirits would find shelter amongst the roots of Litta's people. As she set them afloat she turned towards the fateful eye and sang before it the terrible song of judgment which her people sang only when one had to be condemned to death. It was the song for cutting off a branch from the vine, the song of the surgeon when he was forced to take a limb. Litta sang it to the eye, and all the stars of heaven echoed her singing. The unnatural light trembled, smeared, closed, faded. The fiery eye extinguished its reflection in the river. The tiny leaf-made coffins swirled downstream in the current. Litta climbed up onto one of the slippery stones, and made her way back down the road to the camp.

⌂

There was no one else dead in the morning, nor in the morning after. Nidyom was the last to be mourned. Litta told the story to the Narananti women, but they did not believe her. They wreathed her sayings in silence, and did not repeat them in history to their children. The graves remained: no one knew why they were there. Already a Queen had been appointed from amongst the women. The plans of a city had been drawn out with care. Of the ruined city that had proceeded them they said, "These are good stones. Already cut. We will use them for our building." They filled in the graves with soil, left the treasure undisturbed. The only thing retained was a stone woman, bending over, helpless, to protect her child, which was enshrined, for no reason that anyone could quite remember, in the center of the city that the Narananti colonists founded.

The Rite of the Thaw

• • • • •

"Let me not fall asleep in the lair of the wolf, nor put my head down to lie amongst the bones," Yydra prayed. The snow was falling around her, an unexpected invader snapping its white, frothing jaws at the palm leaves. Yydra's thin cloak had been designed for more clement weather and the loose-woven fabric, painted with the geometric image of an Owl in shades of olive and dusty blue, was soaked through and stiff from freezing. She had been walking for nearly a day and a half without stopping. It was no longer her hope to make it home alive, but to get near enough to civilization that her body would be discovered and ensconced safely in an armoured tomb where she would be able to protect herself from the savage gods that roamed the earth in search of souls.

Yydra fingered the ashes of a handful of lemon bark that she had kept in her pocket in view of emergencies. She had already burned it to appease the sleeping Owl, who had taken shelter in Her old-pocked oak, holding the winds in Her tawny wings. Death was always on the Owl's breath, but when She slept, that was when the worst ravages would come. She would sit ensconced in darkness and look with a half-opened eye on the sufferings of Her faithful, waiting to pick at the jellies of their eyes when they had fallen. She wove a snare out of the tempests, and set it on the path of the unworthy. The dust of Yydra's sacrifice was a reminder that her prayer had not been answered.

The snow slid up the sides of the girl's low-cut boots. The feeling had abandoned her toes, and numbness crept down the long, blue-veined extremities of her delicate arms. Her frost-bitten fingers clutched at the edges of her cloak and tried vainly to pull it across the thin fabric of her dress. The upper winds rushed through the highest reaches of the white-clad trees, whipping them into a howling, lupine fury.

She did not notice the wolf-prints crossing her tracks, and probably would not have been able to identify them if she had. She was accustomed to quieter game – ground squirrels that nibbled on the acorns that had buried themselves beneath the blanketing white, and the stuttered footprints of rabbits that hopped from burrow to bush seeking the last of the berries that hung like dried-out jewels on the underbrush. These berries were not of the sort that is suited to human consumption, yet the possibility of taking a handful, hoping that some dark toxin lurking in their golden-beaded hearts might set her mind flying along the blissful pathways of forgetfulness, had already crossed her mind. She had discarded it. Nature held many terrors for those who faltered within her clutches, and the forest was merciless with its victims even in the best of weather.

It had been a long journey, even before the snows. She was returning, and there ought to have been a pack on her back, filled with soft furs and tender smoked venison. With this she might have made herself an insulated hollow in the shelter of some fallen tree, and nibbled away her profits until the snow passed. But the traders had not come. They were inconstant at the best of times, and when there were dark omens in the sky, strange movements in the weather, unnatural rhythms to the tides, or a twig standing amiss in the center of a salty swamp, they were loathe to leave the safety of their vast savannas. It was understandable. Even now, as she stumbled down the long pathway towards certain futility, she did not blame them for failing to come. Surely they were tucked away in the bosom of their tents, rocking their infant children and hoarding their stash of fresh-killed goods, congratulating one another on the wisdom of having kept their harvest of buffalo flesh and bay-berries buried away to sustain them until the melt-waters came.

Eventually, the land began to fall rapidly, the trail turning and curling back and forth on itself like a white-bellied snake slithering down a hill. The slope was slippery, its marshy banks concealing patches of sharp toothed ices. Several times Yydra slipped, and was carried down, the hidden rocks tearing at her wool stockings until they were nothing more than a set of slightly bloodied rags that trailed behind her, leaving a track of red to summon the scavengers of the woods. She took the knife from her belt and cut them loose. She washed her wounds clean with the snow, hoping the cold would convince the vessels of her body not to disgorge their heady mead onto the trail. The bleeding stopped.

Yydra picked herself up and stumbled down the last few feet to flatter ground. Here, in the lee of the ridge, there was little enough wind, perhaps, that she would be able to nurture a tiny spark into a fire. She sliced away the dried bracken, the bark of a silver tree, the low branches that had died under the shadow of their more elevated brethren. The wood was wet from the snow fall, but she had experience with lighting fires in the rain. Her tinder-box was hidden beneath her clothing, kept warm by her blistered skin. She drew it out, struck a spark. It lay quietly in the palm of the tinder, then, slowly, hungrily began to devour its bed. She tested out the kindling. It caught for a moment, and then, dampened by the snow, began to sputter out. Gently, she blew across the red-fringed blackness that crept across the bark. It smouldered and would not light. Another piece showed the same reluctance. She blew out the flaming tinder, and made a snug roll of the kindling, placing it beneath her shirt, against her skin. Hopefully there would be enough heat in her body to warm and dry it. In another hour, she would try again.

◆

"The Wolf was once the greatest god in all the world. In all the world, I say, and I will tell you why. Because all of the other gods have always stalked about on land, going hither and thither, digging up fields and sowing rain, and they may all be placated in some way or other. Think of it. You wish for the Owl to season your fields with pleasant winds? You burn a stick of hickory and offer up the giblets of a mouse. The Owl will place herself in the service of men for a trifle. Consider the Swan. She consents to have her own kind slain by the hundreds and set on the river. She delights in this. A representation of the blood which she gives so that the crops may succeed. We've had enough of that at our mother's breasts. But the Wolf. Ah. The Wolf is different. The Wolf is not concerned with persons. She does not care if you are a Prince or if you are a dung-heap muck-man. The Wolf's jaws are always open. She prowls about the world and she goes down beneath it, and lives and breathes in the ocean where men will find themselves dead, and she rises up sometimes as high as the sky and bites a piece out of the heavens. Yes, the Wolf may even eat the stars at her pleasure, or scratch them like eyes out of the face of the black. There is no god like her. She is death, and She has never ceased to stalk this land."

◬

A lone wolf walked alongside Yydra. Its eyes were small, its belly sagged. It looked as though it was about to pup, and she almost pitied the creature: it was a poor time of year for food and for young. None the less, there is pity, and there is foolishness. She had armed herself with a long stick and occasionally she rapped it on one of the trees, and scowled at her pursuer, yelling out the harsh, thick cries which contained all the barbaric force of her ancestors. It was an old art, nearly lost, but had once struck such terror into the heart of a foraging bear that the poor creature had stuck its head between its legs and run directly into a large poplar, trying to flee from a mere boy. Or so her grandfather had always maintained. The wolf did not seem to be particularly perturbed. It followed, eyeing her curiously, waiting for nature to weaken her.

Night had grown full, and the belly of the moon was dragging along the horizon, balefully scratching itself on the bare branches of the trees. It was nearly full, and its light was enough that Yydra thought she could see clearly. She did not see the moment that the wolf disappeared. Whether it had gone off to gather more of its kind, or to chase some easier prey, she did not know. It was gone, though.

Her own body was the enemy now. She remembered once being told that if a boy fell in the pond during the winter, and remained there long without being pulled out, his fingers and toes would become as blue as a turkey's gums, and would have to be cut off to prevent the black sickness from rising to his heart. She did not dare take off her boots to test the colour of her toes.

⌂

The Rite of the Thaw had to be carried out on the night before the coldest day of the year. Isha had known this since she was a child. If the rite were neglected, the Wolf would refuse to open her maw. If the wolf did not open her maw, then the entirely of the world would never be drunk down into her belly.

This was the way of it. The way of being at one in the Wolf, and in death, and in the World. Isha had known it since she was a child. It had come to her when she had been made to swallow the fire that kindled her belly and filled her mind with the mind of the Wolf. She had been young then, and it had seemed only to be pain. She had not understood the

82

second child, the way that it had come into her, the moments of suffering and confusion in the night. The old man had taught her a great deal, but she had not understood, even when her body had coughed up a little, half-deformed being – something more like a gill-less eel than like a human being – and she had not known where the strange animal had come from, or how it had gotten into her body, or how the fire had made it come out.

The old man had taught her how to take the creature of her womb to the head of the water, and to put it in the cauldron with all the dried out remnants of the spring, and how to make the broth that could be poured into the headwaters to whet the appetite of the Wolf in the sea below. Then it would open its mouth, and all the world would come alive so that it might pour itself out into the gaping jaws of death.

⌂

It was nearing the middle of the night. The stark shadows carved out by the moon shuddered back and forth in the wind. Yydra was certain that she was going to fall into a drift at the side of the road. She had stopped being able to feel her body, and already had become a sort of breathing spirit, a specter that haunted this road and she wondered if she had been tricked, as the dying sometimes are, into walking on after her body had fallen to death. It did not seem so, but there are things that are difficult to tell. There was no one to ask. She thought of retracing her steps, going back and looking for her body, but it occurred to her that it had probably been taken by the wolf. The image of her leg being dragged through the snow convinced her that if her body was being consumed, she would rather keep on walking until she reached the edge of the world and never know.

It was in the midst of these reveries that she failed to notice the plume of smoke that was spilling gently, gently into the air. The clearing was around her before she was conscious of it, and a little wedge of light was winking out of a shuttered and curtained window. The owner of the hut could not afford glass, but they had worked well in cob, and the snow that piled up on top of the shingled roof had not collapsed it in. Yydra crawled towards the doorstep and beat on the door as hard as she could. It opened, and as warm, brown, woman's hands grasped her beneath the arms and pulled her carefully inside, she realized that she had a body after all, and was going to live.

⌂

"The Wolf is a crafty god, a purveyor of hope. Sit, sometime, at the death-bed of a dying man, and you will understand what I mean. The Wolf circles around, sniffs at the sheets. The breast clutches up in fear, and the sheets are gripped in the dead-white hands. And then...it is gone. The spasms leave the chest, the lungs rise freely, the hands release their burden. A scare. Everyone is laughing, now, and drinks a draught to the health of the old man. The old man himself sits up in bed, laughs, and takes a little of the brandy. He is strong and the sows in the barn need feeding. An ox would not dare die with the yoke on its shoulders. Who thought that he was going to die? He will still be shooting chickens at a hundred and three. Laugh again, and again. Any other god would be fuming. But not the Wolf. The Wolf sits on her haunches, and waits. She has a preference for suffering – recall this always. The old man can laugh. He can weep. This is indifferent. He goes out into the barn, old, tired, and clumsy, but flaunting his recovery. He knocks over a lamp, and everything sets on fire. The old man hides himself in the cellar. There is barely air enough to breathe; all the pain in his chest is back, and there is no brandy, no loving hands to clasp. Nothing. But he does not die. The Wolf was not prowling around his bed because it wanted old flesh to chew on. In the end, it will take the bones, when the flesh has rotted away of its own accord and there is nothing left but a ragged will and a little bit of tough skin. This is what the Wolf throws to its faithful minions, to satisfy a little the eternal hunger in their bellies. But she herself has come for the people in the house. The children that the grandfather clutched as a promise of his future. The infant in arms. These are the morsels that the Wolf craves."

⌂

Isha had become barren. She had made the traditional rites, had boiled the potions in their pots, had ploughed her womb with the herbs of fertility, and sowed it twelve nights with the seed of virgin boys. But the moon had turned itself on her, and in its spite it had turned its face away. The flow had ceased, and not all the beating on the breast of the Earth, nor the tearing out of hair and the weaving of bracelets, nor the mixing of Swan's dung into her stews had brought back life to the garden within. Perhaps it was a curse that all of her children had cast up from the bottom of the sea. Sometimes she saw them dancing around the house, having picked up their little bones from the threshold of the Wolf's cave, coming to dance and dance their mother insane. Shush, she told them. This is not a place for you. You are not to be here, you go back where you are dead. There must be something burned in the fire, something delicate, or else there will be nothing for the Wolf to eat. You shush and go back to Wolf. She is your mother now, and I was never anything. Never anything to you. But they would come and dance all the same, and sometimes they put coins underneath her door with the faces scratched off, and Isha would know that they were all gathered there, at the gates of the Wolf, a little cabal that hated her and wanted to see her dead. But they were very small, and very weak, and it was not a matter for her to consider if they had wanted to see such a thing done to her as this. How it had happened, she did not know, but perhaps they had come and danced for the young one in her womb last year, and had taught it some secret sigil to carve in the wall before it was cast out by the drink of fire, and now it had made the blood stop its flow, even though Isha was far too young for the barren season yet.

But it could not be said, and could not be stopped, and the Wolf had been sleeping a long time, only waking a little bit to drink up the flow of waters from the land. Without that, there would be a great flooding like there had been before, and everything would be drawn down underneath the sea. Isha did not know the history of it, but the old, old man had taken her when she was a girl, and had shown her the old foundations of houses that were swum around with eels, and he had told her that it was because the ritual had not been kept. This had made her quiet. Oh, it had made her very quiet, during the darkening of the moon, and during the rising of the sun. She had learned very hard, then, because she was afraid of the sea, and of the flood, and of the starry eyes of heaven turning all to water, and she was terrified of the Wolf. O! She loved the Wolf, and she was terrified of the Wolf, and now she could feel it in her heart, near as bone, near as stone. She could feel the Wolf moving in, and soon it would be her.

The snow had started falling thickly, and this was evidence that the Wolf intended to let the entire world fall under the spell of water and death. It knew that the secret rite would not be kept, and it was stirring, hungrily in its sleep. If it wasn't awakened it was going to yawn, to yawn, and swallow up everything in its yawn. Death, death. Isha was the

Wolf, was death, and she was going to devour the world. It almost made her happy as she looked with glazed eyes on the frozen stream, and saw how good it was to drink beneath the ice, and rolled her head backwards. Her body was new, and there was going to be everything contained within it.

No. Shush stupid child. The Wolf is in you, but it is not you. Never, never. The Wolf has its secrets and its ways, and it is going to insist on something. It is not time for everything to not be. It is time for another round, another season, another age, another spring. Even when there is barrenness. Oh, the spring is going to come up around these wet, cold hills, and the ice is going to break on the stream, and there will be new things that rise up, and new things to devour, and everything is going to go on, and on.

Isha leaned down towards the stream and she clawed at its surface until a wound broke in the ice and she was able to dip her hand into it. She brought the water up to her lips and it froze them very sweetly. When she had drunk from the pool where all of her children had washed out towards the sea, she turned and went back towards her hut. It was very cold, and the road was winding grimly through the darkness. Somehow it had become night, but that didn't matter. She could live in the night, now. The Wolf was in her blood, and it was going to send her a new thing, and Isha would be death, and someone else would be thwarted birth.

There was a sound. A pounding. Claws or hands on wood. Something had come. There, left on her doorstep, a girl, a gift. She walked up and put strong hands underneath the girls arms. The girl was hardly awake, nearly frozen. So light, almost a child. Isha lifted up the gift, and carried it inside.

A Moral Tale

· · · · ·

In every collection of stories there must be one moral tale which is included in order that the reader may be duly schooled in the virtues and led upon the path of right thinking and harmonious action. This is such a tale. It concerns a virtue which will be counterintuitive to my Metenem readers though it is in fact a deity in Laboria. There is no word for it. The closest thing is "integrity" but of course when you think of integrity this will bring to mind all sorts of associations. You will think of the integrity of a person who refuses to use cheap stone in the repairs of a roadway that was originally made of true-cut granite. The integrity of a woman who will not deceive her husband as to the nature of the sauce in which she has boiled his fish. The integrity of a child who lowers his little head and tries not to cry as he hands over a poorly done assignment, but who treasures in his heart the knowledge that he did not cheat. To a Laborian, none of these qualities pertain. Their god governs only a single aspect of human life and that is the taking of bribes.

Do not laugh. It is true, the people of Laboria really do go to the shrines of this deity and they really do bow before it sweating and scraping crying "O mighty one! O defender of cattle! O keeper of the treasure-boxes! O jewel incorruptible! Please help me this day not to receive bribes or to be swayed in the justice of my rulings by the base desire for gold." As you will naturally infer, such prayers are rarely answered. Those who feel beholden to present themselves before the idol-shrine and to make a great show of their incorruptibility are the very last men that you would want ruling against you in a court of law unless you happen to be very wealthy and capable of offering more gilded ox-horns than your opponent.

Of course, to a Metenem this is most absurd. Metenem do not take bribes. What would be the point? How could you place a soiled coin in the hand of a merchant without immediately giving yourself away? Your shame would flame out through the surrounding air like fu-weed thrown in a fire. The entire marketplace would fall silent. All eyes would turn this way and that, searching the outstretched hands to see whose fingers held the sullied gold. It would only be a matter of time before your eyes would flinch before such scrutiny and you would be forced to drop the coins on the ground where they would be trodden and spit upon by everyone, from the half-breed fishmonger's boy to the most dignified and honourable representative from the Office of the Queen.

It was therefore with a certain trepidation that I found myself on these very precincts, standing just inside the gates with two miniscule gold coins in my hand. It is the practice, in Laboria, to offer the gods a bribe whenever you wish them to do you some small favour, and this practice has not even been abrogated in the case of the deity responsible for controlling the vice of bribe-taking. One of the priests of the cult cast a hungry eye over me, quickly saw that I was Metenem, a scholar, and furthermore a wearer of mended sandals. A man of no account. Or at least a man of meager accounting. He wandered on in search of richer prey.

I was left in peace to approach the sanctuary myself. It was one of those ancient Laborian temples where the god is hidden away in a deep and many-pillared recess. Great carved stellae rose on either side of the pillared hall. One showed a man with fine-chiseled features holding out his hand and keeping at bay a handful of coins which a mendacious and beggarly fellow offered to him. On the whole my sympathy was with the man offering the bribe. The artist had captured his desperation, the ragged dignity of his poverty, the fact that the coins in his hand represented the entirety of his holdings and his last drop of hope. The man of integrity on the other hand was richly dressed and I fancied that I could see a little bit of fattened paunch sticking out beneath his brocade coat. The other stone was entirely inscrutable to a Metenem. It showed some sort of mythical Laborian beast rising from a pool and radiating light over a heap of pyramid shaped objects. I have made several attempts in my life to discover, either through scholarship or through questioning, the meaning of this stone but if you ask a Laborian they will cover their face, bow thrice towards the earth and whisper something incomprehensible before fleeing from you as if you had threatened them with a poxy embrace.

I stood on the lower step of the temple looking up and uncertain of precisely what I was supposed to do. It was a matter of some import. Although the Laborians insist that the stars and the ancestors are the gods of the Metenem, there are important differences. Our temples are simple and easy to use. One enters. There is an oracle or a sage who might be consulted. One states one's business. One is given an answer, and usually assigned some back-breaking and spiritually rewarding work. One may use the quiet of the facilities to meditate. If the stars are pleased with the harmony of these proceedings then their pleasure is a quiet and unannounced affair.

Laborian deities on the other hand are like matron aunts who have never quite given up the hope of one day being married. They must be fussed over and preened and reassured that they are beautiful and eminently virtuous. They must be plied with bon-bons and one must be always wary of the least mis-step in their presence: after all, a smudge on their hem might be the difference between nuptial bliss and everlasting barrenness. I had once had the experience in the past of accidentally offending a Laborian deity by stopping to adjust my sash in the exact spot where the sun glanced off the pinnacle of his shrine and I had spent an entire day bound to said pinnacle in an extremely humiliating posture while the Laborians below very solemnly pelted me with pebbles. Even though the vast majority of the pebbles missed their mark, it was not an experience that I wished to repeat.

Unfortunately, it was not easy to get an idea of how I ought to behave simply by watching the Laborians go about their business. There were various denizens of the temple dressed in a bewildering array of ceremonial garments. Some of them were bearing the kind of gilt gadgets that one naturally associates with worship, others stopped occasionally and adopted odd postures for the pleasure of the god. "Excuse me?" I approached someone who looked like they might be a minor functionary of the temple.

The Laborian fixed me with a terrifying stare, as though I had just made a fart joke in the presence of the King. He raised his entire hand to cover his mouth and then turned and walked on. The tails of his elaborate robes dragged behind him across the marble floor and I was sorely tempted to accidentally tread upon them. I exercised restraint.

"So," I gave up on trying to speak to the natives and addressed the cool shadowy hall in the hopes that my voice might carry as far as the inner sanctuary where the deity dwelt. "I have come." Although I was sure that it was impertinent I stepped just a little ways into the shade of the columned walkways and lowered myself to my knees, feet tucked in neatly, in the proper position for meditation or prayer. I got some strange looks but no one seemed especially eager to tie me to anything.

A cool breeze approached me from the recesses and somewhere in the darkness I could hear the distant sound of chanting and that jeweled, tinkly music that accompanies Laborian worship in all parts of the Empire. It seemed that the god was waiting for me to go on.

"I wish to thank you for the favour that you have granted." This is a very polite form of address in Metenemya, one that precedes the asking of the favour in question.

There was silence in the inner precincts. It was a strangely inviting silence, like the silence of an old woman's sitting room when she has fallen asleep at her knitting. I ventured a little, looking over my shoulder for evidence of irate temple guards. So far my intrusion did not seem to have attracted any attention. I scurried furtively into the shadow of one of the pillars and pressed my back against it. The interior was like a forest of broad-trunked baobabs that someone had planted much too close together. The pillars were decorated with mosaic patterns in shades of blue and silver and they were nearly as wide as the spaces between them. It was an excellent setting for a game of hide-and-creep and I continued as I had started, peering around in the murky half-light for evidence of priests and worshipers, trying not to be seen as I crept from pillar to pillar towards what looked like a sanctuary in the distance.

I was nearly there when my progress was halted by a man coming out. He was wearing a headdress so shockingly elaborate that my brain couldn't even come up with an amusing metaphor to describe it. A ceremonial weapon was gripped in his right hand, sort of weapon that is designed to overawe the fearful with its wicked curves and glittering edges but which would be wholly useless in actual combat. I imagined that in spite of its evident lack of field-worthiness that it would probably suffice for the evisceration of a captive and helpless Metenem intruder. I pressed my back against the nearest pillar and began to edge around it, hopefully out of sight of the imposing figure. I counted my breaths as if they might be few.

The man clanked by, his passage echoing off of the pillars suggesting that he was an army unto himself. I couldn't imagine the purpose of having such a man employed by a temple like this one. Perhaps it was to guard the treasure-boxes and the cattle. These, I might mention, wandered about the complex freely, leaving their offerings on the marble stones with abandon. It leant a breath of the country to the otherwise immaculate precincts.

The bebladed individual having passed me by, I started to breathe normally again and resumed my progress towards the sanctuary.

I reached the step that led up to the inner chamber. Now that I was here I had no idea of what it was that I intended to do. Did I imagine that the god was going to speak to me now that I was nearer to his statue? Did I honestly believe that my little coins would be more efficacious if I dropped them on the ground here rather than placing them in the palm of one of the priests outside? My own behaviour is a mystery to me much more often than I would like to admit. My father says it is my Suese blood that casts a veil of obscurity over my heart. I think it is just that I am insatiably curious.

"Hello," I addressed the sanctuary in a whisper. The walls and the pillars and the carved ceilings and the polished floors and even the golden horns of the cows all picked up my voice and amplified it. I covered my mouth in the absurd belief that I could push the word back inside.

"Hello," the sanctuary answered back. I paled and began to edge backwards.

"I'm sorry," I whispered quietly. "I have judged poorly. I should not be here. I will go."

"You really are a very curious boy." A figure appeared between the narrow, tight-packed pillars of the sanctuary proper. It was very slight. At first I thought that it was a girl, not really more than a child, but as she stepped forward into the dim light of the hall I could see that she was an old woman with the most unlined face that I have ever seen in one so aged. She was wearing a dress so simple and unadorned that for a moment I thought that she must be a foreigner, but no, her skin was Laborian-pale and she wore her silver hair in a circle of knots

100

atop her head which was the style for Laborian women at that time.

"I apologize for my curiosity." I bowed repeatedly in the way that Metenem boys do when they are very sorry and hope that their masters will forgo the prescribed beatings. "Perhaps you will accept these as a token of my contrition." I proffered the two gold coins.

The woman in the plain dress laughed. "Do you think you can bribe me?"

I turned even paler. I was starting to look a like a Laborian myself. "No. No. I didn't mean it as a bribe. I had intended --" I stopped. A good Metenem never babbles. He does not grovel. He stands in silence and considers his words before speaking. I bit my teeth together so that the Suese half of my tongue wouldn't disgrace me. "I have offended you. I apologize and accept your chastisement."

She laughed again. My shoulders had become as stiff as the granite statues in the courtyard, but now they loosened a little as I realized that to her I was a ridiculous figure. "You had better come inside."

I stepped up. The pillars were about five deep, and then there was a small cramped enclosure where the statue of the god ought to have been. The only problem was that there was no statue. There was a podium for the statue to sit on, and several copper basins to hold water for keeping the idol's brow cool, and there was even a ceremonial brush with a silver handle for dispatching any dust or spiderwebs that dared to profane the god's stony face, but the deity itself was conspicuously absent.

To my immense surprise, the woman climbed onto the podium and sat there cross-legged as though she were the god. I very quickly reviewed my studies in Laborian and reassured myself several times over that Integrity was a male god, taking masculine pronouns and masculine endings in every case. I spent several minutes standing there in mute confusion before finally I blurted out, "How ought I to address you?"

She smiled tolerantly. "You may address me as grandmother." To my Suese half this made perfect sense. The Suese address old women as aunt or grandmother indiscriminately, but I was not aware of it being a Laborian custom.

"Grandmother, why are you sitting on the perch of the god?"

"Pish piddle," she said. "The god has been absent from his seat for quite some time and I don't think that he will mind if an old woman uses it to rest her bones."

I gasped. I searched her face. It was not Grandma Bo, I was sure of that. Grandma Bo was large-boned and built like a troll. Grandma Bo had prodigious hands and had been a rider of horses well into her ninetieth year. Grandma Bo's face had possessed wrinkles as numerous as the stars. This woman was completely different. "Who are you?" I asked guardedly.

"The moon, the moon. I am over the moon!" she cackled, letting down her legs and kicking them back and forth with abandon like a small child.

"This is very foolish," I said. "I think I must have taken in some unfortunate substance." I looked around for a censor that might be burning an intoxicating incense. None was readily visible.

"Why don't you tell me what you have come for?"

I gathered myself together. It had seemed easy enough when I was approaching a Laborian statue, but standing in front of a woman who might be flesh and blood and who might be a relation of mine made it different altogether. "I," I closed my eyes and lowered my head. "I --" There was no

103

getting past it. To be afraid of mere words was the apex of cowardice. "I have taken a bribe." There, it was spoken. My shoulders collapsed and I allowed my head to sink even lower but I did not debase myself to the point of covering my face with my hands.

The woman gasped with astonishment. I could not tell whether the astonishment was real or just her making fun of me. "You? A Metenem?"

"I. A Metenem."

"And from whom have you taken a bribe?" Now I could tell that she was making fun of me, and deriving considerable pleasure from my discomfiture.

"There is a woman that I have married. I made her my promises. I am bound by them. But I was told that I should leave her and return to my own country and I was given these coins," I held them out. The gold seemed to burn the palm of my hand as hot as the iron that they use to mark a divorced man in my own land. "I did not do it for the sake of the coins, but I took them."

Her pleasure seemed to have evaporated somewhat. "And pray what did you do it for, if not for the money."

My shame became even hotter. "I am in love." It was a terrible admission. To abandon one's duties and one's promises for the sake of a childish emotion. "To a woman who is probably dead and who probably wouldn't have me if she were alive." I could feel the weight of my un-Metenemness bearing down on me like the weight of the ceiling overhead and I was sure that at any moment my ankles would give out and I would be a disgraceful heap on the temple floor.

"Mmm," the old woman reached out. She took the coins from my hand and rubbed them together between her fingers. A strange glint of glee came into her eyes. "These coins are very heavy for their size."

I nodded my assent. I was glad that they were gone.

"Well you had better scurry on home," she said.

"Do you mean to my wife, or do you mean to Metenemya?"

"Well you are hardly a husband, are you? And hardly a Metenem either."

I sat down on the floor with as much grace as I could muster and stared at her feet. I felt that there was some further question that I should ask her, something that would clarify my situation and rid me of my guilt. It struck me in my musings that although Integrity is masculine in Laborian and genderless in Metenemya, its closest cognate is feminine in Suese. I considered the meanings that it had in my own language. I considered my own unworthiness to be in its presence, even if I had given up those cursed coins. I raised my head in order to make an eloquent address in my own defense but the woman was gone. In her place there was a grey and silent statue with grotesque horns coming out of his head and a hint of cupidity about his tight-pursed lips. He was holding my coins clenched within his stone fingers and I couldn't have prised them out if I wanted to. I picked up the ceremonial brush and removed several cobwebs that had sneaked in under his abundant chin, then left. I didn't trouble to conceal myself this time because it seemed somehow as if it would be appropriate for the priests to bind me up in the courtyard and let the people pelt me with the dung of the sacred cattle. I left the temple precincts unmolested.

The main street of the Laborian capital wound its way along the entrance gates of the temple. The upper road wound towards the palace, with all of the royal apartments and the chambers where distinguished guests were housed. My wife would be up there, sitting down to fresh-ground oats and applesauce, the sunlight falling on her pretty white chin. Her family would be there as well, and all of the machinery of the Empire, its expectations, its prejudices, its traditions. The downward road headed towards the gates of the city, the long road towards South Laboria, the river-boats, the ocean, the harbour, the city of my childhood, the path through the jungle, the dusty goat-track, the winding lane, and Grandma Bo's broken cottage with its softly sagging beams and the mildewy thatched roof where families of otigas made their homes.

I looked neither left nor right but allowed my shoulders to sag like a bag of rice as I turned towards that downward road.

Song of the Victorious Dead

• • • • •

Back before there were men in the world there was Ti-Tiri who was the mother island. She was floating on her back in the sea and looking up at the sky. The sea was warm underneath her and the sky became jealous of the sea and said, "You, Ti-Tiri, get up off that sea. Come live in the stars and be my wife." Ti-Tiri said that she would think about it. Then the sea became angry so it stirred up a terrible creation in its depths. These were the shark-spirits. The shark-spirits came and they tore Ti-Tiri apart. Her body was scattered across the ocean so that she would never be able to leave and go up to the sky. But the sky wept for her, and it is from the tears of the sky that the first spices came and were born on our islands. This is why the anise is shaped like a star and why the cardamom pod is like a tear.

Now these things were given to us out of the body of our mother and we should have known not to go selling them to the men who came from far away, but they came with strange things that did not come out of the body of our island: bright plates, pots that could go above a fire without breaking apart, and many other wonders that we could not count. So we sold them the tears of the sky and we worked for a hundred years and maybe a hundred years after that to fill up the holds of their ships with the gift that we had been given.

The ship landed early on the day when our great journey began. I was going to it with a fine bag of coriander jostling along on my back, crush-crunching as the seeds settled themselves against my shoulder. All of us men were dreaming about the bright pots that we would take home to our wives and about the big hams that would brighten our chimneys and put strength into our soups. Our mouths were full of this feast as we were going down into the hold and this is why we did not notice how it was that no one was coming back out.

The sun was still filling up our eyes when we got down inside the hold. This is why we did not see the men who were waiting there. "Be quiet," said voices of

110

men that we could not see, "or you will be killed." Then they pushed us down onto benches, tight close together like fish packed in oil.

We did not say anything because we thought, these are sharks that have come dressed as men from the company. But they would be found out soon enough and the directors who looked over our spice plantation would shoot at them with the big cannons until we were set free. We did not know then that the men from the company had sold us, and that the crates that had come up out of the ship had not been full of smoked sausages and fine rum for us but of silverware and indigo for the plantation directors.

So there were no cannons. Instead, after a long time there was a whisper that came down along the bench and said, "We must make a warning. They will not kill us all. When the hand is squeezed, yell." Some hero had turned and given this whisper to the man next to him and it had gone all the way to me. I turned and told it to the next man, and I could feel how his hand went cold, and knew that he had cramped up with fear. The whisper had stopped with him and it was a gamble now to guess how many people it had passed through before it stopped. Still, when the squeeze came to my hand I started shouting to make a warning for those who were coming in from outside.

Only five of us shouted. The sharkmen came swarming up on us as though the sounds coming out of our mouths were like blood poured on the water. They beat us on our shoulders and our backs and our stomachs. When the other men saw our courage their chests were filled with the shame of a man who does nothing. They shouted to let that shame out and turn it into honor.

It was a very short time after that that we felt the board begin to rock beneath us and the boat pitching as it turned out to the sea. The long lines of benches down in the hold were less than half filled up and this was the way that we counted our victory. But the sharkmen made us count it very dearly and learn to stop our tongues behind our teeth. We who had started the little rebellion were hung up on the walls like we were carcasses going to be smoked. Then they beat us while instructing the others in the dangers of disobedience. We were very proud when they were beating us and everyone was very proud for us. We could hear our friends quietly mumbling out the prayers as though we had been the ones chosen to enter into ecstasy at the harvest sacrifices.

To suffer a great deal is to enter into the great journey. When we were taken down, and the sharkmen had finished clamping irons around our wrists, and had left us in the dark, then the oldest man told us the stories. He told us about how the god of the pepper bush went down into the very darkest place in the earth, and made war on the worms, and how they came up and ate out his heart and he suffered in this way for seven years. He told us how Ti-Tiri heard at last how he was suffering and sent up a great fire to eat up the worms, and this is why there is fire in the heart of the pepper seed, and why this fire has the power to make a boy become a man. He told us the story of the great fish who slumbers in the depths of the ocean, and how the fisherman sunk a thousand golden hooks into his flesh, but he could never be caught, and each place where he was hooked became a golden scale, so that there is no fish like him in the world and he is worshiped everywhere. Through these stories we knew the sickness in our bellies from the rocking of the boat, and the sickness in our skin from the bugs that lived on blood, and our sorrows for having lost our wives and children were just the beginning of a transformation.

After a time we stopped, and we thought, Ah, it is finished. We are going to rise up out of the bottom of this ship like a frog rises up from the mud when the rains come. But the sharkmen came and they told us that we had to be quiet or we would be beaten again.

Then we understood: they still wanted to fill up their hold and they had come to another island to do it. So someone shouted the way that a man does when he is about to go into battle, and all of us began to beat our feet on the floor, and to shake our chains, and to howl so that the men who were on this island would be warned away.

When the sharkmen saw that this was how we were going to behave, they went out of the hold and left us down there alone. After a while, we heard the sounds of loud explosions outside, and then, later, lines of men shuffling down into the hold tied up with ropes. Some of them had been cut, and one man had a hole in his arm that was bleeding very badly. The sharkmen came down and looked at it, and then took the man up out of the hold, and whether they sent him home or threw him overboard as an offering to their brothers in the sea, we never knew.

That night, when they came down with pots of the thin porridge that they had been feeding us, they gave it all to the new men. To us they gave nothing, and they said that we would not get food until we had sworn on our gods that we would be quiet the next time that they stopped at an island. The sharkmen did not realize that it is the custom amongst our people that no one may eat unless everyone eats, and so the new captives

114

ate only half of their portion and handed the rest over to us. We were going to get weak, though, eating only half a portion of this bland stuff every day. We talked this over amongst ourselves throughout the night, but we could not come up with a solution.

◆

"We are going to fast." The old men declared this on the next day, when the food was brought down and there was not enough. "We are going to fast so that we will be given a vision of how it is that we can get away from this place, and back out into the world where we will be human beings."

So the older men did not eat, but looked into the inner blackness and waited for the inspiration to come. The rest of us filled ourselves as well as we could, and sat there with our bellies rocking back and forth in the waves.

"Why don't we just promise that we will be quiet," said that man next to me, the man who had been too afraid to whisper that first day. "When we are loud, they only beat us and starve us, and it does not do anyone any good," and he pointed to the new captives, who had been rounded up with violence because they could not be rounded up with trickery.

One of the old men opened his eyes and looked very hard through the darkness. He said, "If your tongue is cut out of your throat, then you find a new way to speak without a tongue. A man who does not speak when there is speaking to be done might as well be a mollusk." Then he closed his eyes again, and this was all that was to be said about the matter.

◆

So we resolved at the next island to be very loud. To give us courage, the new men told stories of how they had fought against the sharkmen, and of how some had escaped, and how sharkmen had been wounded and perhaps killed. This was also when we learned how the men from the company had betrayed us, and so we understood that there was no hope of being saved except by our own kind. Then we all felt that if we were very loud this time, and truly woke up the monsters in the bottom of the sea, then maybe the people on this shore would know the danger before we even got there, and would be able to come and rescue us out of the dark belly of the ship.

So as soon as the sharkmen came down and ordered us to be quiet, we started to bang at the planks, and to sing our songs, and to call up the great fish. But they had just been fooling us, to see what we would do, and we were not really coming to an island at all. When they saw our courage, they went around and they picked out all of the oldest and weakest men -- men

116

who were our fathers and deserved the peace of gray hair -- and they told us, "Now you will be quiet, or we will kill these ones."

But the old ones looked out of their hunger and there was a light far down in their eyes. One of them began to sing that song of the victorious dead, the song which men sang long ago when they were going out to battle, before the company came, when we had truly been human beings. Then we understood that this was the meaning of our journey here, and that we had become these things-in-chains in the moment that we had put aside our own leaders and our own customs, and had sold the tears of the sky to the company. We, here in the bottom of this ship, were as the heroes of old who went down inside the whale in order to learn there the secrets of strength by which human beings became masters of bone and fire. We were here, and we were learning again the secrets of strength, so that we would go back and teach our people to be truly human beings, and filled with might.

The men who had suckled at the breast of sharks put the old ones to death, then. Our old ones went like a bride goes to her wedding bed, with their hands raised up and a song of joy on their lips. And we rejoiced for their lives, and that the great ones had looked on them with such favor, and had granted them

that they should finish this journey in glory now, before
further sufferings came to wear wrinkles in their brows.

⌂

When we came to the next island, the sharkmen
did not come and tell us to be quiet. Instead they played
a different trick, going ashore in small boats and
bringing men back so that there was nothing that we
could do to give a warning.

By this time, many of us were getting sick, and
some were beginning to die from it. All through the
night, you could hear moaning from those who had the
sickness, and although we still told our stories with
great courage, in our bellies we were afraid. The sun
who fills men's blood with its heat and gives them
courage, had not looked at our faces in a long time. We
had started to think that maybe there was nothing else
anymore except to be buried in the bottom of this boat,
and to die. There were very many who lost their hearts
and began to weep, like women do, and we turned our
faces down towards the floor so that we would not see
this shame.

A long time passed. One morning I woke up,
and the man next to me, the one with no courage in his
heart, was leaning on my shoulder, dead. The sharkmen
came and took him out to feed to the sea. From then, I
could hear his spirit at night time, shivering and crying

to itself. I tried to tell him, "Go on, go from this place," but his heart had gotten so cramped up with fear that he couldn't make himself go on. Even when we sang the songs of the dead and stamped our feet to scare away the spirit, he stayed there, and his fear began to spread into our hearts as well.

◢

I think it was about the passage of two moons before the ship finally stopped and the sharkmen came down and told us to get out. We were taken out into the sun, but it was not a sun such as we had ever known, and not a world such as we had ever seen. Truly, we had journeyed into a different realm, and it was full of mountains that had been made by hand, and of springs that shot up out of the mouths of stone beasts, and other wonders which we had no words for describing. They marched us through this, and it was very difficult because our legs had not been made to stand in this kind of world, and were very weak for it. They gave us good food and strong meat, and we understood that we had come across the long way that only the dead are supposed to pass.

We talked about it amongst ourselves like this, "We cannot stay here. We are still living, and it is not a land for us. Look how our legs are weak here, and how our stomachs, no matter how hungry we are, can take little of this food." And so we resolved that we were going to have to go and see the gods who were in charge. The men here were dressed in fine clothes, even richer than the men from the company, and they covered their faces with pictures of the faces of angels and devils, with jewels around their eyes and curls made out of gold instead of hair. From this we knew they must be servants of very great gods, and dared not to show their true faces in the presence of such powers. We were going to go to those gods and explain to them that we were very grateful for the things that they had taught us, and that now we wanted to go back and tell these things to our people.

This is not how it happened. Instead, when we were fed, we were made to exercise, and when we had exercised, we were made to lie down and sleep, and we did this for several days, until, under the sun and with the food of the gods in our bellies, we began to get strong again. Then, just when our strength was nearly renewed, we were taken out to a place in the city and put up on a pedestal so that all of the people could come and look at us and see the transformations that had taken place on our journey. At least, this is the thing that we thought was happening, because in our homes, when a man is put on a platform, it is because he is a hero. We were filled with pride, and tried to break our chains to prove the renewal of our strength.

The chains did not break, but there was a great ritual, with many calls and responses, and after a time the first of the heroes was taken out of his chains and sent with a fat man who wore a gold and purple face. Some said, "There, they are taking us home to honor us," but then some of those who had thought longer about it said, "No, they are selling us. They think that we are pigs." And this, it turned out, was the truth of the matter.

◆

After that day, we were no longer together. Each of us was taken to a different place, and there are, I think, probably many stories from the men who were on that ship, and mine is only one of them. Perhaps the stories of the others are better and more worthy of being told, but a man can only tell the stories that he has and not the ones that he doesn't have.

My story is that I was taken and put in the back of a cart. A man got in whose false face was dark blue, and polished like the night sky, with eyebrows of burnished silver. There was not a single piece of his true body that was showing, and it made me wonder whether he was a man at all, or just a spirit that had clothed itself in the manner of a man. But he had with

121

him another man who covered his face in a face of white, without any decoration, and who had true hands, and who spoke to me in the same words that the men from the company use. They had chained me up in the back, and after a while they brought a girl and put her next to me. She was very beautiful, not in the way that women are beautiful, but in the way that a sika deer peering out of the forest is beautiful. Her face was much paler than our faces, and she had a tangle of hair the color of copper.

We left the place with the buildings like mountains, and we came out into a path that led through the true mountains, which were much taller than anything I had ever seen on my island, and which put the man-made mountains to shame. It was then that I realized my mistake, and I saw that the gods lived out here, and that the people had only made up buildings in imitation of the true spirits. But these were not the gods of my home, and I did not think that they were very likely to give me an audience, now that I saw how high and forbidding they had made their fortresses.

After most of a day, we stopped and the man with the white face got out. We were, it seemed, going to make a tent for the blue-faced one out of some tapestries that were rolled in the back. I got down and I helped to put up that tent, and when it was done we went out and the white face took food out of the wagon and went in and spread it out in a feast. The girl was given a decanter of wine and was told that she was to go in and serve at the hand of the blue face, to make sure that whatever he required was given to him. She smiled, but there was, I thought, something very wrong with her smile, and then she went into the tent with the wine and did not come out again.

I was given a thin blanket and told to lie down on the ground. It was cold here, and I felt that the cold was going to come up into my bones and steal away my life. The white face lit a fire, and that gave some help. Then he made a bed for himself from a pile of skin and went to sleep.

It was very dark. I turned my face up to see the white tops of the mountains which were all around us. They looked very hard and unforgiving. This is the steep way, I told myself, and understood the vision that had been given to me. It is the way of suffering that ends in victory. I decided that I should not sleep, but keep vigil and pray to know the spirits that lived in these parts. I saved a little of the food that had been given to me, and I threw it into the fire so that the scent of it would go into their nostrils, and they would know that I intended friendship. They came and gathered on the other side of the fire, swaying like thin flames, plumes of smoke or icy winds. I recommended them to the great fish, and to the spirit of the clove tree, and to all of the other local gods of my home. But they did not have the body or the appearance of the spirits which I knew, and I could not tell what they intended to do with my prayers.

After I had kept vigil many hours, I heard a cry coming from inside the tent. It came from the lips of the woman, and I understood, then, that this was what I was supposed to stay awake for. My legs were still kept together by chains, so it was going to be very difficult to move with stealth. Still, I could see that white face was sleeping, and I had become very strong through all of the things that I had suffered.

I crawled slowly, holding on to my chains so that they would not rattle much, and I made my way over towards the tent. There was a struggle happening there, and I knew what sort of a struggle. There had once been a man from the company, who had got the idea into his head that he could come and take over the right to the womb of one of our women. We had all heard her cry out, and we had gone and cut him in pieces and given him to the fish. So I knew what sort of thing this was.

But when I got into the tent, the blue face was not up on top of the girl holding her down. She was on top of him, like a hunter on top of his kill, and she was drinking deeply out of the decanter of wine. For a moment I thought, You fool, you have come to the rescue of a whore, but then she brought the decanter down from her lips, and shattered the mask of the blue face.

She must have noticed the movement at the curtains, and she looked at me. I looked at her, and understood that she was killing this man. So I went over and showed her that he was not yet dead. I took the chains that were around my legs, and we twisted them around his throat. I pulled until we were both certain that the breath had gone out of his throat. She took off his broken face and hung it across her chest, like a necklace or a breast-plate. Now we could see his true face: it was very ugly, with teeth that stuck out too long, and a nose that was curled upwards like a pig's. All over it was covered with red pock-marks, as though he had been ruined by some disease.

"The white face is going to wake up," I whispered. The girl did not understand me, but I pointed outside, and made the gesture of a man sleeping. She nodded, went over the chest where the blue face kept his things, and found a knife. After she

125

went out and I heard a very soft cry, the cry of a man who is surprised. She came back, and started to work at my chains. When I was freed, we took down the tent, rolled it up, and put it in the back of the cart. We rolled the bodies of the masks over the edge of the mountain path, and I could see the spirits of the mountain down below, smiling as they received our sacrifice.

"Now," I said, "we have come up into the mountain and defeated the evil. It is time to go home and bring news of this to our people," and I pointed down the path that we had come by.

She shook her head, and explained something to me at great length, with many gestures that I did not understand at all. She pointed in the opposite direction, up the mountain path. I was very sad when she did this, because I had felt certain that I had earned the favor of the gods and that it was time that I could go back to my wife and to my children to bless them with the strength that I had gained through this trial.

But a man cannot argue with his fate: he may either succumb to it, or be overcome by it, and that is all. I climbed into the front of the cart with my free limbs. She climbed in beside, and took the leather chains by which the beasts at the front were put to service. She pulled on them, and we began to ascend the mountain.

126

⌂

It was two days later that we were overtaken. There were thirteen men like the blue face, with masks in various colors to cover up the ugliness of their true bodies. They rode up and surrounded us, and spoke in words that neither of us understood. We were overpowered very quickly, for they had swords and wore strong armor, whereas we had nothing except my chains and the knife that she had taken from the blue face.

They killed the girl first. Laying her down on a boulder that jutted out of the mountain's face, they put a knife into her chest and cut out her heart. The rest of her body they threw down the side of the mountain, but her heart they kept, and passed it from one to the other until it had grown cold. When all of the warmth had gone out, they put a sword through it, and put it over a fire. They kept pointing towards it, showing it to me.

I nodded. I understood that they were telling me about the value of the heart, and about how a man may still have all the fires of courage burning up inside of him when he dies. I understood too that this was why they had passed her heart around between them, because they had no courage in themselves, and this was why they had to send thirteen to capture one man and a woman. They were trying to make the courage

127

from her go down into the hands, so that after this they would have more strength.

They did not kill me quickly. That is the way to kill a woman, out of respect for her body, and for the sufferings that she has in birth. They killed me very slowly, so that throughout my death I would be able to show the heavens again and again the strength and the courage that they had taught me. I sang the song of the victorious dead, until they cut the tongue out of my throat, and then I sang it in my heart. That song was still there in the last breath that came out of my lips, and it went up into the mountains, and the strange spirits there received it with joy.

This is why if you come up on this mountain, on a day when the sun is clear in the sky, you hear it still, that song, echoing between the peaks.

River Brides

· · · · ·

The streets of the Laborian capital were clothed in mourning for the King. Garlands of green silk and blood-lily festooned the buildings, long lines of choristers sang dirges on the streets, incense poured from every Temple doorway, and tearful supplicants spouted poetic elegies begging heaven to return him to the throne.

The Queen was exhausted with all this public mourning. It was three days since her husband had been poisoned, and the necessities of the funeral had kept her constantly in public view. Decorum demanded a perpetual flow of tears, a frequent descent into hysterical sorrow. Her eyes were red with stinging nectars that she had applied to freshen her grief, and her fists were sore with pounding the ebony roof of his casket as it was carried into the tomb.

Now, at last, the well oiled hinges of the ancient sepulcher had closed on their treasure of rich perfumes and royal bones, and she was allowed to rest. Lest her grief become a burden on her people, she had begged leave to go and weep her torrents alone. She kissed her only son good-bye, and climbed into a litter of rubies and acacia to be borne away through the city streets. The people threw themselves onto the moon-stone pavement before her, convulsing in new ecstasies of sorrow. They begged her bearers to trample over them, that they might share some fragment of their beloved Queen's burden. They slit their wrists and poured their blood out in the streets, and swore on all the gods of all the heavens that they would shed it to the last drop to find out who had slain their King. The Queen smiled bravely through cayenne-scented tears, and reached towards them like a dancer stretching towards her love. Then, as she approached the monastery on the river, she pulled the curtains across the door, and leaned back against the cushioned seat.

The monastery perched in silence over the river: a marvel of engineering worked so that the virgins living there would not have to sink posts into the bosom of their watery husband. Wrought of marble and gold-gilt wood, it spanned the deepest currents of the stream. From its center there curled a golden ladder, so that the river's wives could descend to bathe by night. Surrounding the monastery, a high hedge of cedars protected them from outside eyes, and a circling fence of iron kept trespassers from the sacred grounds.

Within its walls, all was quiet and smelled of stone and water. The Queen removed her royal robes – the layers of silks and feathered embroidery, the stoles of fur and the jeweled crown, until she was dressed as a river-bride, in robes of plain beige that fell loose and long so they would always drag along the dust. "I shall be in the chapel preparing myself," she said, "send Mother whenever she is ready to see me."

The chapel was a hall of golden wood whose stained-glass portals looked down on the river below. The sun was slanting from the west, through a bank of windows devoted to the sorrows of the river-brides. The Queen knelt, as she had done forty years ago on taking her vows, before the first of the stained-glass icons. All was told and foretold in those images. The current that had brought her here was mapped, and she could see where the water flowed ahead. She looked up, silent and tearless, on the stained-glass portrait of seven slain men, and a woman drowned at the river's edge.

⌂

"I shall not marry, though a hundred men come to bear me away. I shall not leave your waters. My demon. My love."

This prayer had been intoned a thousand days when the first of the suitors refused to be repelled. Loyala was adamant that she would not marry: the demon had come, and founded the city, and the city had prospered as none in the world. The demon of the waters had always flowed through it, and washed all ill-fortune from its shores.

Like all maidens, Loyala had been consecrated to the river in youth. She had thrown the flowers of girlhood on the current, bathed naked to wash away her menstrual flow, drank deep of the waters that made the womb blossom. But it had not been for Loyala as for the others. The river had not merely cleansed and prepared her for marriage. It had

132

entered her, held her in its icy arms, and had taken her for wife. Now, though dozens of suitors implored her, she would not consent to marry any man.

It was while she was bathing, at the setting of the sun, that she became aware that she was being watched. There, on the bank, a man that she had turned away that morning sat amidst the blowing reeds, with a lute laid across his lap. When he saw that she had seen him, he began to sing; a love song that seemed blasphemous as it carried over the waves. She submerged herself, and held her breath until her lungs began to ache for air, and in the grip of self-inflicted death felt wholly united with her river-love. Before the blackness overtook her, she begged the river to swell his banks and devour the man who had come to steal his bride.

She emerged on the surface, blue-lipped and gasping, the thin air violating her lungs, her ears filled with the sound of sacrilegious strumming which she realized too late played only in her mind. A second later, the hands that had plied the lute were around her waist and she was being dragged, naked, to the shore. There, on the smooth stones, she curled herself up and mumbled soft curses to the pebbles and the waves. The suitor knelt beside her, his hair falling across her face like a net, his lips breathing out heat and false perfume as he placed his hand on her flesh to feel for a pulse.

The river did not rise and swell his banks. He gave his wife a greater gift than that: a rock that he had not smoothed but sharpened, a means of defense that dug suggestively into her palm as she rolled over to hide her face. The strength of the river still filled her body, and with the speed of a white current frothing over stone, she overturned the man who had dared to fish her from the waters and sank the rock deep into his skull.

The river eagerly bore the body of his rival out to sea, and tenderly cleaned his wife of all stain, so that she emerged pure and unbloodied, and when the body washed up on the edge of the harbor it was said that such a blow must have been delivered by a man of terrible strength, so that not an eye was turned towards Loyala's slender hands.

It was thus that she learned to spread a net for the importunate. If a single refusal did not suffice, she would send a note saying when she could be found bathing, and if the suitor dared to come then she could sink herself beneath the water and wait until he came to bear her out. He would die then, before he ever left the water, always with the same stone which she saved in a secret hollow of the river's breast.

There were seven killed before she was caught. Since she had been a Hero's daughter, they did not hang her, but locked her in a tower, looking over an endless plain of grass. Not a stream, not a lock of her lover's hair, could she see winding across that deathly green, and she wept rivers in memory of her loss.

Thirty years passed, and she was no longer a girl, when word came that the man who had fathered her was dead. He was to be given a Hero's burial, with a rich armory taken down to the grave, and as he had no other daughter, and his wives were all long dead, Loyala was allowed to leave her captivity to bestow the final kiss. She did not weep for him, this father that she hadn't known, but all the while looked out from her chains to see her husband's body snaking beside the road.

It was so long, then, since her crimes had been committed that though all recalled that she had murdered seven men, no one could recall the cause. So when she begged to be allowed to wash herself in the river, to be free of the dust of travel when she came to her father's tomb, they saw no reason to refuse. They lengthened her chain, and turned away their eyes, and told her to beware of going out too deep. Although she was more than a mile from her childhood home, she knew at once what shape the river bottom would hold. She could see the little hollow where the water dipped deep: the place that he had prepared specially for her. Silently, tingling with the touch that she had nearly forgotten, she walked through the water until she reached that place, then deflated her lungs entirely of air, and dove beneath the surface. A moment later her husband filled her as he never had before, rushing into her lungs, and taking her completely for himself.

⌂

The Queen stood and kissed the pane of blue-glass that showed the river carrying his rivals out to sea. "I shall not leave you," she said softly, "though a thousand men come to bear me away. This I vow, on all my life."

The meditation complete, she took four steps backwards, her slippered feet brushing softly against the wood, and then proceeded to the next of five. Carved in glass, the beige-robed women leaned towards the street on hands and knees, groveling in the hope of receiving alms.

⌂

Not all who wished to wed the river had a Hero for a father. Not all had suitors lined at their doors to seek their hands. And so they went out into the streets, for the river could not grant them shelter and they were not yet ready to receive the final consummation. They would take their hair and brush the ground before them, pouring out little streams of water onto the feet of passers-by and then raise their hands to receive a coin. "The river's blessing," they would say quietly when the coin was given, and then return to begging as before.

It was in that time that the maledictors first began to work in the marketplace. The rich would wrap themselves in peasant's clothes, and pour dust on their heads so the gods would not recognize them, then they would slip into the darkened tents and for a fee, would have their enemies cursed. If a place on the Council of Heroes were opened, the mighty and renowned would slink to the hut of some ill-spoken sorcerer, and before the dripping candles, proffer some little scrap of paper on which the names of their foes were written, and would turn it over to be cursed in high and dreadful words and then be burnt to ash. Celebrated playwrights would arrive in the costume of lowly actors, and whisper the name of a play that was to run that night, written by some despised rival, and would sometimes even script the heinous doom that they wished to see called down on the performance. Noble ladies would borrow clothing from their chamber maids, and since they dared not say the name of the woman they thought had been in their husband's bed, they would bring a fragment of the adulterous sheet and have that burned instead.

The business was ill-respected, but well paid. Not a single event of import in the city went unaccompanied by a long line of hissings and sputterings, chants and invocations of doom. But it was very expensive, the business of damnation, and though charlatans abounded to take a peasant's money, only the highest and noblest could afford the true maledictor's words.

It was thus that one of the women brushing the street with her hair was asked if the river could curse as well as bless, seeing that he had countenanced murder and dragged his rivals off to sea. The story told seemed worthy enough: a man wronged by an adulterous wife and a lawless fiend who had played to be his friend. A poor man – poor as the mendicant river-wives were poor – who could not afford a maledictor's curse. A man without the power to smite the fiend, and without the heart to cast away the wife. "Yes," said the river-wife. The river was a demon, powerful as any the maledictor dared to name, and he could curse as much as bless. So for a little coin pressed into her hand, and couple of words whispered on the street, she wet the man's feet, and then poured water on his hands so that he might not be held in guilt, and then uttered the river's curse on those who had wronged him.

What doom was wrought by the curse, the river-wife was never let to say. It became a strict rule among their number, that whatever curses were whispered in their ear by day, as the evening sun went down on the horizon, they would bring all the weight of accusations to the river side, and for every curse that they had promised, they would take a stone and put it in their mouth, and then, with a mouthful of stones, dive into the river and disgorge their load. After that, their tongue would be forever silent as to whom had asked a malediction, and against whom it had been uttered, and if they later learned of its success, this too would be dropped to the river bottom in silence.

⌂

The Queen picked up one of the stones that lay on the sill of that particular window. They were used rarely now, but kept there, in memory of the power that the river still possessed. She whispered a name very quietly, and placed the stone on her tongue. Then she pressed her head against the floor and brushed it with her hair, before crawling on her knees to the next of the windows, where a river-wife lay prostrate before a knight, her beige robes torn, and nearly dead with weeping.

⌂

"Let it be passed, as law before this council, that should some poor maid fall into the clutches of the demon river, it shall be considered not a crime, but a mercy – indeed a duty of the soldier of the realm – to break her marriage by whatever means he might."

These words had been spoken and posted in every barracks in the Realm, passed by the Council of Heroes itself. It was now a long time since the river-wives had poured out water in the streets, since they had openly offered their blessings to the feet of travelers. Long had they been forced to hide in the forests, to be sought after only by the desperate and depraved. Visits to their husband had become few and dangerous, taken only on the holiest nights, according to a secret calender, so that they might not be found and imprisoned for malediction. They knew at once that the force behind this new edict was none but spite: a woman had recently fled her engagement to a Hero's son, and had joined herself to the river by night. Now the jilted young man had been seeking her for weeks, and had caught up to her on the river's edge one sacred eve, and with twelve men to support him, had borne her away. When the law was passed, they had no doubt of what was happening on the distant estate from which they had no power to rescue her, and they wept and filled their mouths with stones, and spit out curses, not only on the Hero's son and his men, but on all the Council of Heroes who had countenanced this terror.

Since they could no longer go in public wearing their beige robes, they had taken to hiding the robes beneath ordinary clothing so they might pass through the markets, past the stalls selling spices from distant islands, past the orators piling praises on the heroes of the day, past the women who bowed before each other like idols in mutual adoration, to the poor little troughs where they would trade an ounce of blessed sand for a handful of beans and a cup of stale grain.

It was on such a trip that the river-wife Miserera, who was beautiful – as many river-wives were not – passed by a group of soldiers, with a little length of beige cloth trailing in the dust beneath her skirts. They did not trouble to follow her out of town, to drag her into a darkened thicket, or to make a pretense of what they intended. The writ of the Council hung on their barracks wall, and they knew perfectly well by what means a marriage to the river might be broken. And so they seized her, and took her to the fountain, which was fed with water from the river, and holding her by the hair with her head half-way submerged, they stood in a circle, taunting the demon to rise out of the fountain and protect his wife. They stripped her of her outer garments, and lifted her beige matrimonial robe, and when they had finished violating her they threw her into the fountain with cheers and laughter, and poured wine over her, calling it an oblation to the cuckold.

This was by no means the first such assault since the law had been made – nor, in fact, had the soldiers confined themselves to the wives of the river. Any maid dressed partly in beige, or with her skirts dragging in the dust, might be thought to be a river-wife, and it had become impossible for girls or their fathers to seek vengeance in such cases. It was exceptional only in that it had been undertaken so flagrantly, in full sight of so many people, where mothers had to drag their children away from the marketplace, and where a young man whose great-grandfather had been one of the greatest Heroes of old, happened to be standing by. He helped the girl from the fountain, and took her from the city, and sheltered her in his home at a village for retired Heroes and their sons.

Miserera would not be comforted, and in her lamentations, the young man saw a means by which the corruption that had fallen on the Hero's Council could be brought to an end. Along with other young men descended from true Heroes – from men who protected and did not turn the innocent over to the cruel – he assembled a new order: the Knights of Justice. On horseback they would go from village to village, bearing Miserera in her stained and torn beige gown, and she would fall on her knees in the streets before the fountains and would screech and tear at her hair and call on all the streams and rivers, all the wells and lakes, all the ponds and marshes, to rise up and avenge her, then would fall weeping until sunset, when her body was wracked with so much sobbing that the Knights, fearful that she would kill herself with grief, would give her some brandy and find some friendly house where she could sleep.

It was not her beauty alone, or her sorrow, that stirred up so much ire in those who saw her. The abuses of the Council were becoming many. The soldiers plundered fields like common thieves. They took men's wives and threatened death if a word were spoken about it. They demanded ransom in return for leaving merchants unharrassed. Much anger already stirred throughout the Realm, but Miserera's cries galvanized that anger, and the ranks of the Knights swelled, and their supporters grew in number, until, carried on the flood of a victim's tears, they marched towards the city in the night, and slayed the Heroes of the Council, and the Generals of the Army, and put the soldiers to the sword, and filled the river with blood.

◊

The Queen had no further tears to spill. There were certainly enough of them being poured into the river today – and soon enough there would be blood as well. A white haired King who died upon his sheets could not expect to leave this world without some challenge to the throne; a little shedding of a little blood, a fitting tribute to the line of him who died. But for a King to die at the greatest of feasts, before all the nobles of the Empire; for his chokings to echo through the hall, above the circling musicians and cries of dismay; for a King to fall while gold hair still mingled with the gray, with the tell-tale spots of poison on his throat – such a death would unleash a flow of blood to drown the city. It could not be otherwise. It was only a matter of time.

In honor of her fore-sister, whose tears had bled the city clean, the Queen prostrated herself and tore a small clump of hair from her scalp. She left this before the window, with a pile of other strands, and then proceeded to where a lone woman, in foreign gown, lay pinned to a bank of clay, her stomach cut open, thronged around by river-wives bent to the ground with tears.

◬

The monastery had been built in the years following the abolition of the Heroes' Council and the establishment of the throne of the Kings. For centuries it had been the only home of the river-wives, and they – no longer pariahs, but now ladies of a powerful house – had attracted many young brides from amongst those who wished no worldly lord for husband.

For the crime of intruding on their sanctuary, or of peering between the trees to see them bathing, a man could lose his eyes, or hands, or head. An order of river-guardians had risen up to stand *in persona fluminis*, their eyes always turned towards the outer world to shoot down any intruder on the river's harem.

When Fidelia had gone down to bathe in the middle of the night, to share the private joys of communion with her husband, she nearly cried out when she saw the stranger swimming towards her. Had she done so, a great deal might have gone differently, and a dozen arrows might have sunk into his back, but there was something in the way that he approached, in the way that he held his finger to his lips, and in the tone in which he whispered that caused her to pause.

"Who are you, that you dare to intrude here?" she demanded, whispering.

She could not see his smile in the darkness, but felt it like a secret. "Woman! Know ye not your own husband? Can you not feel by my breath, and the coolness of my touch that I am none but he?"

Indeed, his touch was cool – not threatening or invasive, a hand laid on her shoulder, nothing more. "If you lie, and are only a man, I will tear your member from your body and feed it to my lawful groom," she whispered vehemently.

"If you would do less, I would drag you beneath my waves and bind you there and lash you with weeds, and never allow you the peace to die. But I would not have it that you be deceived by a soft tongue: I will offer proof. This river is but an image of the True River. This water, but an image of my body. I will show you my true form, and then you will know me for what I am." He took her hand then, and with something between mistrust and desire, she followed him up onto the darkened banks. He led her by long and winding paths that stretched beyond the gates and the cedar hedge – though they encountered no obstacle or gate – and emerged at last by the side of a river such as none had ever seen before. In idyllic splendor it curved between two high red banks, jeweled with the red-fallen leaves of autumn, and at the same time, with the silvery-pink petals of the spring. Trees in the hues of every season grew along the banks, and above, on the opposite bank, a palace of clay and glass rose into the sky supported on a forest of shining beams.

Though it had been the middle of the night, the sun here shone at its apex, and she blushed to look on his nakedness and to know that he looked on hers. But there could be no doubting the truth of his words: such a river could exist only in the vales of the gods, and only a god could have revealed it to her.

He took her, that night, to his bridal chamber, where the ceiling shone like a field of stars, and in the morning, he took her back to the monastery beside the worldly river that was only an image of his true form.

At his bidding, she summoned the other river-brides, and night by night, they allowed themselves to be led to the palace by the side of the true river, and there were given a new home, where neither night nor death ever fell. Some would not receive their husband in fleshly guise, and left the monastery, going back out into the world to live as paupers and beg in the streets. The river-god did not object: he would not have any unless they were willing to have him.

For a hundred years, they lived that way, in the valley: joyful when he came to them, and otherwise always awaiting his return. Other wives came and joined their sisterhood, and it became known that the river-god was none other than the King – or at least that when he walked on the earth, amongst the cities of men, it was as King of Laboria, and nothing less.

But there was one wife who came and was not willing to have him, though she said not a word of it to anyone. A foreign woman, from a conquered land, she had been rescued from the ruin of her city as a girl, and now that she was grown into a woman it had seemed only fitting that the King who had saved her would take her for a bride. She offered no objection, but on her wedding night, with the waters of the river still fresh in her hair, she had taken the sheets of her wedding bed, and strangled him to death. In the bridal chamber they had found him the next morning, cold and still as a constricted pond, and though they bathed him in tears, and set him in the waters to heal him, nothing would bring him back to life.

They had taken her then, and pounded stakes into her hands, and driven them into the red clay-cliffs, and then they had sliced open her stomach and left her writhing guts exposed to the merciless sun, and they had thrown themselves on their knees, weeping for their slain husband, while she groaned and screamed through the hours of her agony.

◇

The King they had laid in the tomb that day had been an impostor – it had been known, now, for a century, though none dared to speak it aloud. The Queen had been given to his successor – the now late King of Laboria – in order that none would suspect that it was known. She had undertaken this defilement from loyalty to the river; as much as the woman pinned to the cliff had suffered marriage in order to slay her people's conqueror. "We are very much the same," the Queen said softly to the dying image. "Even if you hailed from a distant land." Truly, this had been her sister, and not the deceived, beige-clad adulteresses who had given themselves up to the wiles of a deceiver-King.

She stood. She could hear the Mother of the river-brides' slow step on the floor behind her and she turned. "It is nearly finished," she said. The last window was of plain blue panes, awaiting the last image of the river-cult's sorrow. "The second will be much more difficult than the first."

Her spiritual mother nodded slowly and looked through the colored windows down onto the waves. She did not say anything. Both understood that when it was done, the Queen would not need poisoned drops to draw out her tears. The line of the impostor was nearly ended. Her husband, the King, was dead. There remained only her son.

Ocean of Sand

• • • • •

Vydhunas' village was in the middle of a vast desert, built inside the calcified remains of an ancient leviathan, surrounded by the rotten-tooth stumps of dead mountains. When Vydhunas had been a boy, he had always pictured the leviathan as a giant camel, and had wondered at the image of its head rising up into the sky, almost high enough to meet the burning pin-prick sun that drove everything except the monsters inside during the day. But on the morning that the Guardian came to determine the futures of all the boys and girls in the village, he learned that a leviathan was a huge fish, which was something like a tadpole that never turned into a frog.

"Does that mean," he asked, "that there was a pool here, as big as our village?"

The Guardian smiled with the ineffable sadness that always lingered around the eyes of those who bore his office, "You see the desert?" he said, and all of the children nodded gravely. "God didn't make the world for deserts. An ocean is a pool bigger than all that sand put together. Stretching out further than you could walk. This thing..." And he patted the huge, stone rib-cage over which the patch-work camel's hides had been stretched. "...didn't wriggle in the mud. It swam." Then he knelt down and drew a picture of the big fish in the packed-down sand.

Vydhunas' mind was not able to encompass it. He had seen the rainfalls. He had seen the frogs come up out of the mud like the dead rising from their graves. He had seen the pools where they laid their eggs, and he had joined the other boys in digging those pools deeper, in laying out camel-skins to hold the water in, trying to keep the tadpoles alive just long enough to sprout their legs and transform into frogs. It was a sacred duty, an image of the human soul being readied for heaven. But he couldn't picture water that spread as far as the red dunes and distant mirages.

⌂

The Guardian was an old man, and it was said that there was nothing in the world that he hadn't seen and didn't know. There were, however, things the Guardian would not talk about. If you asked him about the world outside the desert, or the city – which was something bigger than a village – where he had come from, then the hollow in his cheeks would sink a little deeper, and he would frown under his mustache, and get a look in his eye like men got when another baby had been lost to the heat. "There is knowledge," he would say, "that men can't bear, except if God helps them. You don't go asking for that kind of knowledge." Then he would turn the conversation to the cactus crop, or look at the toes of the newborns to see if they were plump like boiled beans, or dried out like pepper-corns.

When it came Vydhunas' turn to have the prophetic stones thrown, he was called out alone into the desert. The sun was sinking behind an endless fringe of dunes, and he was told to kneel down in the dust across from the Guardian. "What do you mean," said Vydhunas, "about the sea? I mean – is it something that exists now? Or is it something from the holy books? Something from before the world was corrupted?"

The Guardian looked up sternly. "Does God unmake His wonders just because you and I don't care to obey His laws?"

Vydhunas blinked in confusion. He was not yet sixteen years old, and though he could tell when the distant succulents were in bloom by reading the stomach contents of a gazelle, he did not know much theology. "I thought He made the world dry up because of our sins."

The old man raised an eyebrow. "You good at keeping your lips together?"

Vydhunas nodded.

"Well let's cast the stones, then. See what they have to say about the future of curious young men. Hmm?"

Vydhunas swallowed and knelt very straight. There were other mysteries in the world beside leviathans that could swim in oceans, and distant cities were maybe hundreds of men could live together without dying of thirst. Vydhunas was nearly old enough to take a wife, and though sex was hardly kept secret in such a small community, he understood that it was like the holy wine that the Guardian brought once a year from the Temple: a greater thing than it looked. It was also perhaps the only thing that the Guardian knew little about – not even as much as the silly girls who had taken their husbands a year ago and who thought that marriage conferred on them the dignity and wisdom of the Crones. The throwing of the stones would determine whether Vydhunas would spend his life like the Guardian, or whether he would be allowed to take a wife. It would also, most likely, determine whether he would live to stretch his grey beard to the ground, or be killed in the endless war against the monsters.

The Guardian drew a sign in the air and asked the spirit of God to preside over the ritual. Then he reached into a bag of cracked leather and drew out the stones. They were strange stones, neither red nor bleached grey, but dark and impregnated with a silver sparkle, as though they were a faded image of the night-sky. They were also hard and smooth, as though they had been ground within the wheels of heaven, and they had a sheen like twilight shining on an ephemeral desert pond. Each one was marked with one of the fourteen names by which the Benai'i knew God, and only the Guardian knew how to read them. He muttered a brief prayer in the high language of the Temple liturgy, then, with muted reverence, he dumped the bright stones out into the dust. He sat for a moment, staring at them, scratching at the cracked wrinkles on the side of his head. Then he looked up, his head cocked to one side, and gazed at Vydhunas.

"What does it say?" Vydhunas asked quietly. He did not know if he was allowed to speak, or whether there was some kind of magic in the stone-reading that took time to take effect.

Squinting, the Guardian shook his head, then stopped, and nodded slowly. He looked as though his long beard might be concealing laughter, and Vydhunas felt that the old man was toying with him, deliberately making him wait. He lowered his eyes. It was not good to think such things about holy men.

The Guardian cleared his throat noisily and said, "What do you want it to say?"

Vydhunas shrugged very slowly. His body had started to want a wife, but he had been playing Sentinel from the time that he had been a small boy, and he knew that the greatest and most important work was to rid the desert of the monsters.

"You know," said that Guardian, "this used to be an ocean. I told you that earlier, but I didn't explain myself fully. You see, our friend there..." He pointed to the leviathan's bones. "needs a lot of water to live in. This wasn't the edge of the sea. This entire area used to be deep under the ocean. Water so deep that if you'd been standing on the bottom, you could have mistaken the surface for the sky. Can you understand that?"

Vydhunas shook his head. It was like heaven – something too big, too wonderful, for the mind to contemplate.

"Good," said the Guardian, "you'd have to be a proud idiot to think you did. But you can see the edges of it, right? Like a mirage at the edge of your soul?"

Vydhunas nodded.

"All of this used to be an ocean. It dried out because the monsters came. Not here – not the middle of the water. They came to the beach, where the water meets the land, and God pulled the water away from them. They followed the water, and God pulled it back some more. The monsters didn't come here because they wanted to live in the desert. The desert was left behind as the monsters advanced."

"And if we get rid of all the monsters?" Vydhunas asked, images springing into his mind like flowers after the annual rain.

The Guardian breathed out a little smile, "They say," he said, "that since we came here the rain has fallen longer. More of the frogs live every year. Less of the children die in infancy. I think it's fair to take that as a sign of what is intended for this place, if we fulfill our vocation."

"And mine?" Vydhunas asked again.

"Do you think I'd have told you all this if you were going to stay home and raise camels?"

⌂

A second boy was destined to be taken from Vydhunas' village as a Sentinel that year, and he would have been if it were not for the stranger who came while the Guardian was out in the desert exposing his head to the sun and praying for the village to thrive in the coming year. The stranger was not like anyone that Vydhunas had ever seen – a tall man, with skin so white and full that thick beads of water dripped out of his face. The sun, filtering through the gold and black tapestries of his camel-borne litter, had painted large swathes of red across his corpulent cheeks. He was the owner of three camels, but he did not know how to look after his animals properly, and Vydhunas disliked him immediately just because of this.

160

The stranger spoke to them in a strange, slow accent, like an adult speaking to a child, or a bully drooling at an idiot. But his words did not matter. What had mattered were the things carried by the other two camels. The first bore a great chest, which the biggest boys were instructed to take down and open. The second was covered in bags filled with liquid, and these the wet-man himself distributed to everyone in the village who clamoured forward. The older children reached him first, and then the younger ones, and then the adults, and finally the elders got up on their creaking bones and tottered out into the open, shielding their eyes as they tried to find out what was going on. By the time that they had decided to forbid anyone from receiving the stranger's gifts, the chest had already been opened, and the skins uncorked, and everyone was too busy staring and babbling in wonder to hear what the elders said. The stranger invited them to eat, and drink, and they feasted themselves on the ripe, plump fruits – figs and dates and pomegranates, oranges and bright sour lemons, little red berries that burst on the palate like frog's eggs, and in the skins, wine, stronger and more heady than anything that the Guardian had ever brought from the distant Temple.

They bit into the fruit in wonderment, and then passed them around, savouring each drop of juice, giddily inviting the others to take a bite, until at last the chest was empty, the wine-skins drained, and all the faces of the people flushed and bright and ripe for dancing.

They invited the stranger into the village then, and since even the old had tasted a little of the honey-coloured wine, there was no one to protest too loudly. They brought out the wheel-harps, the bells, the bone-pipes, the brass horn, the copper mortar and pestle, the cymbals and the steel pipe: all of the sacred instruments with which they worshiped God. They played a song of rejoicing and thanksgiving, and danced until they exhausted the sun's wrath and it sank beneath the far-off red horizon. Then the stranger spoke of more such fruit, of barrels of wine and rivers of honey. Such a tale he spun that all leaned forward in rapt attention, their eyes glossy with long unsated yearnings.

When the Guardian returned, he looked at the stranger and at the empty chest, at the scattered wine-skins and the children sleeping in their plates of beans, at the girls who were soon to be married laying across the chests of men who were not yet their husbands, and he spoke a single word. In a voice as terrible as a sandstorm and deep as the ocean where leviathan had once swam, he thundered, "Laborian!"

It was a word known only as a foreign fable a terrifying breath of a distant world. He might just as well have accused him of being a demon from the innerworld. The Guardian spoke to the stranger in a tongue that no one had ever heard, a terrible tongue like the hissing of a serpent, a tongue that sounded like poisoned honey. When the stranger answered, he did not sound like he addressed an idiot or child, but except the Guardian, no one knew what had been said. Their voices rose, their anger grew. Water ran in rivers over the fat man's face. The Guardian's eyes burned like dawn on the mountains.

At last the Guardian turned to all the waiting people and said, "Each of you, get yourself a stone. As large and sharp as you think you can throw."

The people of the village paused. None of them were called to war. They had never thrown a stone. And they knew that if they obeyed, the stranger would never come again, and in all the long and weary years of life, they would never taste another pomegranate, or drink another draught of such fine wine.

Vydhunas, however, pictured the ocean. He pictured the desert transformed by rains. He pictured the silver-bushes putting down long roots and raising up a shade in the hottest part of the year. He pictured trees jeweled with fruit. He pictured children ripening in the women's wombs, and always milk enough to feed them. He reached down into the cooling red sand and picked up a stone – good and heavy.

Slowly, the others followed his lead. They stood in long ranks, holding their rocks, and the women pulled the children back and hurried them off to bed.

But not a single stone was ever thrown. The stranger was not willing to become a martyr to whatever god had led him. He did not argue or defend himself, or threaten violence, but only grumbled in his own tongue as he loped towards the camels and galloped away.

The next morning, as Vydhunas was readying himself to leave the village forever, they found a camel missing, and Zolskas, the other young man who was to become a Sentinel, had disappeared in a long line of tracks following the stranger into the west.

Vydhunas and the Guardian followed the stranger's tracks for three days. Zolskas was a boy of the desert, soon to be a man; much water and many years had been spilled into his life, and the investment was not to be lightly squandered.

The road stretched on unending, occasionally meeting a cross-roads where four tall bone pillars, the length of a camel's thigh, were driven into the dust to hold aloft the golden thread – the Holy Hunter's net which spanned the desert and created safe paths for the Benai'i to walk amongst the monster-infested sands. The same thread stretched along the side of every roadway, it circled every well and hidden reservoir where the Benai'i could safely drink. The Benai'i had been sent to the desert to perform this dangerous work: the building of a new road meant meandering into the open desert where a Sentinel had only his office and his prayers to protect him.

Many times as they were riding, Vydhunas was aware of the monsters watching them from behind the dunes, waiting for them to make some little foray off the path. Their bodies were bent and ruined, and they dragged themselves along the ground like wounded dogs or half-erect snakes. Vydhunas knew that they were blind, that they followed the evidence of sound and scent to find the Benai'i riders, but he still felt himself watched by their wasted eyes.

On the second day, as they were riding down the road, a gust of wind lifted a cloud of red from a nearby valley and carried it, swollen and swirling, across the path. At first Vydhunas thought it an insubstantial monster, a rising spirit, or a Serpent's breath. But as it whirled around him, he could see that it was made of a thousand red petals, sharp as snake's tongues, rolling in a cloud of red-gold dust.

"Signs of war," the Guardian said, and since Vydhunas did not understand, he explained: "This is how monsters make war on one another. They sprinkle petals instead of spilling blood – blood's too precious to waste. Then they negotiate the number of the dead, and they exchange their children's lives instead of soldiers. The casualties are always the most beautiful and innocent – they believe that if they consume the virtuous, they'll gain their virtue. In reality, it means the virtuous never survive, and the monsters grow more monstrous with every generation."

"Do you mean to say they're human?"

"Not as us. They're Laborian – or rather they are of the same kind. Their bodies reflect the state of their souls. It's not so easy to recognize evil amongst ourselves."

Vydhunas looked across the dunes, at the slinking, malformed faces. He remembered the stranger, and wondered at how far evil had removed their forms.

At noon on the third day, they reached a covered stone reservoir in whose deeps the wondrous stuff of life surged from within the earth. They poured a little on the desert as an offering to God, then deeply drank of the cold metallic fluid. As they were drawing up a sackful to fill their water-skins, Vydhunas noticed a figure lurking amongst the dunes on the other side of the thread. It was naked except for several ragged scraps; a woman's body grotesquely distorted, with breasts that hung nearly to the ground and a sagging stomach that dripped down over misshapen thighs. She was covered in blisters, with larvae writhing visibly beneath her skin. Her eyes were blighted creases in her pockmarked face, and she felt her way across the sand with rough, splayed fingers. A bundle of rank cloths was pressed against her breast.

Immediately Vydhunas fell back towards his camel, prepared to leap astride it. He had heard that monstrous women would sing songs that shattered ears, that they could intoxicate a man with a dizzying incense, and that when he had been lured off the path, she would dangle her body obscenely above him like the succubus spirits that haunted the night. Men so enchanted were found with their guts devoured, their vital fluids sucked dry, left to feed the carrion-eaters that crawled out when it fell dark.

The Guardian shuffled towards her with one hand outstretched. For a frozen second Vydhunas clung to the reins of his mount, then leaped forward and grabbed the old man by the arm. He stubbornly dug his heels into the sand.

"Don't be a fool," the Guardian whispered, slapping him aside. "Look what she's carrying." They were nearly at the path-side now, and Vydhunas could smell her scent: something between putrefaction and heavy musk. The Guardian bent down to her level, squatting on thin legs.

168

The woman sniffed like a rooting animal, then held out the dusty bundle of shoddy rags. Vydhunas saw that inside was wrapped a baby: recognizably human, with little open slits revealing cloudy blue eyes.

Since they had no common language and the woman could not see, the Guardian hummed soothingly and reached towards the baby. In the second that his hand crossed the golden thread, Vydhunas saw the trap: the infant was a lure, to trick the Guardian into reaching across the boundary so he could be dragged into the desert and devoured. Vydhunas reached for the Guardian's robe, and grabbed it at the same moment that the monster seized the old man's wrist. But there was no resistance. The mother did not pull. She lifted his hand up towards her lips and held it there, smelling it, then darted out her swollen, purpled tongue and licked the salt and red-dust from the palm.

The Guardian remained still. A second lingered. Then another. In Vydhunas' imagination, the woman bit into the old man's flesh and her sharpened teeth relentlessly and feverishly sucked blood from the wound. But after a few moments, she dropped the hand, and lifted the bundle, holding it out towards the golden line that she herself would never be able to cross.

The Guardian took a little handful of the sand of the road, sanctified by the feet of the Sentinels that had trod on it. He sprinkled it over the baby's chest, and drew the name of God above its heart. Having thus blessed it, he took the baby in his arms, and as he stood, he sprinkled a little of the blessed sand on the mother's head. She writhed and recoiled as though in pain, then skittered back, like a spider on broken legs, and hissed at him in a wounded-snake voice. The Guardian let the blessing he had hoped to grant her drop unspoken from his lips, and he turned towards Vydhunas, holding the baby against his chest.

"She knew enough to want something better for her child," he said. "Let God have mercy on her for the rest."

They bathed the baby, and said the prayers that would deliver it from the worms already burrowing beneath its skin. Then they wrapped it in fresh cloths, and tied it to Vydhunas' back. Mounting their camels, they turned towards the west.

⌂

At just before twilight they came to the edge of the desert. There, along the shore of the dried-up sea, thin gold-green grasses waved in the pale sand, and the air was sweet and rich like rain. Several trees crooked their shadows over the waving green, their branches hung with ripening purple olives. Behind them, the sun stretched out mild, honey rays that burnished the tree-tops like polished copper. Vydhunas could barely breathe amidst such beauty. He did not see the flickering campfire that had been lit in the middle of the field until the Guardian pulled quietly aside him and pointed towards it with a darkening eye. "You go ahead," he said softly, "and try to bring him back."

Vydhunas edged out into the grass. It was soft and fine and whispered against the camel's heels. Slowly, he wound his way towards the fire, trying to fix his attention through the thick mead of moistened air. He drew close and dismounted, and felt the grass soften like a spring beneath his feet.

Zolskas, the deserter, stood beside the campfire in the posture of a cobra, while the Laborian tempter slept behind him on a quilted mat.

"You know who I am," said Vydhunas softly, holding out his hand. The two had lived all their lives in the same village, had grown up there as boys, but Vydhunas feared that some enchantment hung over the other boy's mind, that it was filled with confusion and mirages like a man who drinks the juice of horn-lips and falls prey to the madness held within.

"I'm not going back there, Vydhunas," Zolskas's voice was harsher here than it had ever been in the searing desert winds. "Why should we have to starve all our lives, with paradise only a few day's ride away?" Vydhunas saw that he was holding a knife, not a Benai'i knife, but a foreigner's blade, inlaid with some sacred substance that shimmered with all the colours of the setting sun. "God damn me for it, but I'm never going back!"

Vydhunas swallowed a mouthful of the sweet air, and set his lips against each other hard. Then he carefully undid the knots around his waist and shoulders, and tenderly lowered his bundle down into his arms. He set the sleeping infant gently in the waving grass, then stood and said, "If you kill me, at least look after him."

"What is it?" Zolskas demanded, taking a step half-forward.

"The reason," said Vydhunas, "that we have to starve and fight." Then he explained about the

172

monsters, and their wars, and how they ate their children, and why the ocean had been dried up by God.

And while he explained, and Zolskas eyed him warily, the Guardian quietly crept around behind the fire and came to where the Laborian lay sleeping. He prodded the foreigner sharply with his staff, and with a mewling cry more fitting to an infant than a man, the Laborian woke and started fumbling for his knife. A second later, he remembered that he had lent the blade to the Benai'i boy, and he began scuttling backwards like a crab towards the desert.

Immediately, Zolskas turned and sprang towards the Guardian, and just as swiftly, Vydhunas leaped up on his back. They fell together in the cool gold-green grass, and they wrestled with each other as they had done as boys playing Sentinel and monster back in the sands outside the village. Vydhunas was cut a little before Zolskas lost the knife, and one of his punches gave the traitor a bloody nose, but in the end Zolskas struggled free and followed the fleeing Laborian.

Vydhunas sprinted after him, but by the time they arrived at the olive tree where the Guardian's mount was tethered, they saw that the Laborian had

173

made a terrible mistake. He stood at the edge of the desert, just on the other side of the golden thread, and with a madman's self-assurance was gesturing the Guardian forward, taunting him to follow further into the red sands. Zolskas, with a strangled cry, tried to warn him back, and Vydhunas scanned the hard-baked dust for the shadow of a monster lurking in the dark.

It was not a monster that brought the Laborian down. With a voice like a river breaking through a dam, the Guardian thundered, "Be you now accursed! Execrated, anathema, cast out from commune with men. May the net of God be turned against you, and bind your evils where they cannot harm His people." With this, three times, he smote the ground with his staff, then picked up a handful of dust and blew it towards the Laborian's face.

The foreigner laughed, and burbled some rank nonsense, but next to Vydhunas, Zolskas had turned bleached-bone pale. The Guardian knelt on the ground, his forehead bent to the soil, and prayed silently, ignoring the Laborian.

A minute passed, and the cursed man stepped towards the golden line with all the hubris of a usurper rising towards his throne. He had nearly passed out of the desert, when suddenly, like a man who sees a flaming spirit standing in his path, he stumbled back and covered his eyes for fear. Sweat poured from every facet of his face, wriggling like larvae across his flaccid skin. So terrified was his expression, that Vydhunas expected him to fall at once, clutching his heart within his breast, and die on the spot of fear. But instead, with a half-human cry, he turned and hurtled off into the sands.

The Guardian rose. His face was pale and dry, and his eyes sparked like a lighted star as he trod towards Zolskas. He snorted curtly at the young man, then, with a wave like a knife-thrust, ordered him to follow. Zolskas slunk, defeated, across the grass until all three were standing by the fire. The Guardian ruffled through the Laborian's abandoned treasures and drew out a length of bright-red silk. He laid it across Vydhunas' hands, and told him to stand and hold it aloft.

Vydhunas and the other boy understood immediately what was meant: the red sash was a sign of excommunication, and once it was bound around Zolskas's waist he would never be allowed to return to his people, to take his meals amongst friends, or to lie down in a village of his kin.

The Guardian spoke quietly, with great sorrow, but no warmth. "You have turned your back deliberately on God. You have abandoned your people and your calling. It is you who have chosen to cast yourself out."

Zolskas, whose knees had been weakening in the silence, now lost himself entirely and fell kneeling on the grass. "P-p-please," he stammered, "Wh-whe-where...where am I to go?"

"The path you have chosen." the Guardian said sternly.

"I-I'm sorry," said the young man, and Vydhunas could see all the splendour of the stranger's fruit, of the blowing grasses and the distant oceans, dying in his eyes.

There was a second of silence, and then the sound of tearing cloth, like a garment rent in mourning. As one, Zolskas and the Guardian looked up. Vydhunas had torn the red sash cleanly in two. The excommunication could not be continued. He held the pieces, trembling, expecting to be rebuked for foolish false compassion.

The Guardian took the scraps of fabric with a smile and twinkling eye. He held them out towards the kneeling boy. "You've been offered mercy," he said, "do you accept?"

With all his heart, and with a joy surpassing wine and dates, Zolskas seized the torn up fabric and threw it on the flames.

As the threat of excommunication burned, the Guardian went on. "You'll never be a Sentinel," he said. "But there are other Benai'i out in the world, and this child needs to be cared for. There's no way he'll survive in the desert. Not enough water. Not enough milk for our own. You wanted to go out into the world, and that's where your vocation lies for now."

Zolskas looked down at the monster's baby and didn't say a word. He understood that this was the cost of forgiveness.

The Guardian picked an olive and sat munching it, staring into the fire. Vydhunas readied the camels with a heavy heart. He could understand now, at least a little, how difficult it must have been for this old man to have lived all his life amongst fruit and water, and now to voyage out into that dry, red sea. He twisted his bare toes in the grass for just a moment. The Guardian stumped over to the

Laborian's litter, and emerged with a number of heavy bags.

"You'll need this," he said, dropping one into Vydhunas' hand. It was full of shining golden discs, marked with strange symbols, and the head of what might have been a man or a god. "The Laborian won't have much use for them anymore. You can take his camel – though sooner or later, you'll need to trade it for a horse. You'll find a stream, just a couple miles west of here. Follow it down to the river, and the river to the sea. You've got enough coin there to get a ship to Nida's Harbour. The Priest there can tell you the way to the Temple."

Vydhunas snapped his head up and blinked like a newborn wondering at the sun. "But I'm supposed to be a Sentinel," he said.

"Did I tell you that?" asked the Guardian.

Vydhunas' brow ruffled, and he stared down at the ground. No, he supposed. It had not been clearly said.

"To tell the truth," the old man continued, "I almost doubted myself that I'd read right. Thought I might have knocked a stone over without noticing it. Or imagined what I saw. But for now, at least, your vocation isn't in the desert..."

"What then?"

The Guardian smiled softly and reached under his robes. He drew out a little copper axe, the image of the Guardian's symbol. He hung it ceremoniously over Vydhunas' neck. "Show them this. For ten years – perhaps even twenty -- until my earthly term is done, you'll travel the world, and learn what you need to know. You'll feast yourself on lamb and oranges. You'll see the ocean, and the leviathans spouting. You'll see the city, and the multitudes, and the Temple feasts. Once a year, I'll come to see you – when I'm home to get the wine. And then, one year, God will make you ready, and I won't come. They'll stick my bones under an old sand dune, and you'll be sent back to the desert." He nodded, with a twinkle burning in the back of his eye.

Vydhunas lifted the copper axe a little from his breast. He could hear the faint whispering of running water in the distance. He could see the grass stretching in waves of shimmering gold until it met a smudge of deeper green on the horizon where mysteries, like pomegranates, waited to be plucked.

To Devour the Stars

• • • • •

The albino girl had not always been deaf, but her hearing had been taken from her in the first days of her life. This was why she could not tell what was happening when the strange men with chaotic swirlings of alien tattoos marring their sun-dried faces pulled her from the toppled cart and forced her down in the dirt. They held her head down so that she could hardly breathe and she could see nothing except their feet pounding the dirt in a slow strange circle that widened and closed like the mouth of a fish.

Over the scent of damp earth and rainforest, Veyjtum could successively smell urine and evacuated bowels, blood and sweat, then fire. Once, as she struggled, she managed to lift her head enough to get a glimpse of what was happening. Her foster father was lying unnaturally ashen and still with something that looked like worms crawling through a mass of blood at the back of his head. She realized that it was his brains; his skull had been cleaved by one of their attackers' obsidian-toothed clubs. Her body convulsed and she vomited. After that she couldn't smell what was happening anymore and she no longer tried to look up.

She knew that they were going to kill her. Their feet should have been white but were cracked and tattooed, the cracks filled with black dust. She knew the dust to be the ashes of her people: entire villages, men and women, their children, and all that they owned. This was why her people called them the Wind. Because they came without warning, and when they had blown through a settlement nothing remained to show that there had once been civilization in the wilderness. It would not matter to them that she was a girl or that she was only thirteen. To them she was the enemy merely because of her race. She closed her eyes and wondered why they hadn't killed her yet.

When they let her up there was nothing but ashes. Her foster father, their carriage, its driver, all of her clothing, her books, everything was burnt. They took crude shovels and sifted the ash for bones or teeth, and counted every one to make sure there was nothing missing. Then they took the hammers from their belts, and smashed and pulverized the bones into a powder which they threw into the air in wild ecstasy. Their lips mouthing foreign syllables, they stamped on the still-warm coals and drove the last remnants of the man who had raised her deep into the dust.

Veyjtum could not see why she had been spared, unless it was the color of her skin: whiter even than theirs, white as the palace cranes. But her features were obviously Metenem. They could not have been deceived about that.

⌂

She was learning to differentiate between them by how far back their heads were shaved and by the erratic designs woven in ink and scar across their faces. There was one in particular that she had grown to hate: a man not quite as old as her foster father had been, completely bald, with a mouthful of teeth like rotten black figs. He carried a staff from whose crooked end a long tooth of obsidian hung with tufts of stolen hair. His body was white and bent and it shook with a sort of palsy as he grabbed her wrist and pulled her up the mountain path.

Although only thirteen she felt sure she was the stronger. As soon as they had rounded a bend in the black-purple stones of the old volcanic path she tore away her hand and kicked his shaking legs as savagely as she could. It was the first time in days that she had done anything except be led about like a drugged sheep, or cry. The old man was caught off guard, allowing her to escape.

The sharp-edged palm fronds cut her as she plunged into the underbrush. She could see no clear path in the dizzying, mosquito laden darkness. Her freedom lasted less than a full minute before the strong hands of younger men seized her and she was dragged foaming and kicking, out onto the path. They laid her face down and held a snake before her eyes. She watched its tongue flickering in and out, its jaws yawning, teeth bright with drops of venom. It was a kind of snake she had seen drawn in a book, and she remembered that it does not take long to die from its poison. When they saw that she understood how it was deadly, they took its head and beat it in with a rock. Then they whipped her with the fresh-killed body. The serpent's tail was far sharper than she ever could have guessed, and it plowed her back with painful furrows into which were sown the seeds of terrified obedience.

When she was pulled to her feet again she felt she could not walk, but when the bald-head with the staff seized her by the wrist again she forced herself to stumble after him up the steep path.

He led her led into a cavernous chamber the ceilings and walls of which were painted in the image of the night sky. Her mind traced the familiar outline of stars, and for a moment a pained joy struck her breast. The stars were full of meaning; the letters of the alphabet, and the names of her people, and all the secrets of the universe were held within their patterns. But as she studied these foreign walls, as torches were lit to make everything clearer, she saw that the entire sky had been transformed. Alien constellations lacking grace or balance mangled the image, teeming with terrifying intimations. There were messages written, but she could not decipher them, and she felt sure that whatever they predicted, it was death.

The bald seer led her from wall to wall, showing her pictures that she could not understand. He spoke and pointed and gesticulated and struck the wall with his staff. The welts on Veyjtum's back were starting to tighten. She strained to do what was wanted of her: to know what it was that they were trying to tell her.

One wall showed the earth as a consuming mother who brought forth monstrous-looking animals and then devoured them again, her legs locked in an obscene embrace around a man whose head was the moon. On the next was a beast entering the bed of hideous woman. Something half-black, half-white was growing in a womb as round as a planet. The seer pointed repeatedly to this image then hit Veyjtum in the breast, drawing a line like a simple constellation, between the fetal image and herself.

She gagged and shuddered and turned away. She could not disprove the obscenity; she had never known her mother. She knew only that she had been abandoned and that before being left to die her ears had been destroyed. This was the only legacy that was left to her by the woman who had borne her.

The seer grabbed her shoulders and pulled her down so that she was kneeling beside him in the middle of the chamber. On the dusty floor he traced three figures, each an image of Veyjtum. Two lines extended outward from the child towards two older selves. One was bathed in a glow of radiance and men fell before her worshiping. The other's body was broken, full of tangled lines, and the constellations were dissolving at her feet.

Veyjtum stared at the images then wrote in the dust, *I don't believe in your prophecies. I don't accept your image of the sky. My world is something different.* She stared at him, and in spite of her defiance her lashes trembled. His throat wobbled strangely as he looked at the characters she had written. It was clear that he could not understand a word.

⌂

She would not eat. It started as a matter of necessity: grief and fear had robbed her of her appetite. But when she began to understand what they wanted, she refused not only food but water as well.

On the second day the pangs of thirst began to drive her mad. Everywhere she saw nothing but

187

water. Her ears, which had heard nothing in thirteen years were suddenly filled with a mad-crashing-rushing, an eternal thundering which she recognized without understanding why. This mirage of sound falling on dead ears was relentless. Even the vibration of her screaming could not drive it away. She writhed and held her blighted ears and wailed. They held her down and forced a pitcher between her lips. The water it contained was infused with some noxious herb. Clamping her lips shut, she struggled to be let up but was too weak. They pried her teeth open with a knife that cut her gums. As the water trickled down her throat the world resumed its long quiet. Then, as she lay in a stupor of moral exhaustion, they pried her lips apart again and forced in ground-up rice, stroking her throat so she would have to swallow. She lay on her side and stared out the doorway at the hillside, at the stone amphitheater where their sacrifices were held, at the two pillars which the seer had taught her were supposed to hold up sky from earth. She dreamed that she held those two pillars chained to her body. That the strength of her hatred was so great that she dragged them down, and all the world collapsed in blessed darkness.

Waking she found the world had changed. She vaguely recalled a dream about riding, and she could see horses tethered to the dead-tree stumps nearby. Below, a plain of red and thirst spread out around a huge basin at whose margins lapped wide rings of crystal-salt. In it was a green-blue sea devoid of life. They led her down to it; the last of her resistance was gone. The seer was there along with a younger bald-head, thin-limbed and spindly, covered in wild tattoos. Together they laid their hands on her head, her shoulders, her stomach, her legs. Wherever they had touched her, a stinging like a nettle jostled through her skin, though she did not try to escape.

When they finished this the women came, heads bowed, obedient. They bore long strips of binding cloths, the sort Veyjtum had seen used when the warriors came home to bury their dead. Laying her on the ground they wrapped her up, binding her arms against her chest. When it was finished she could not move limb or finger. Then the men lifted her and bore her towards the salt-lake. Like a larva being sucked from its cocoon she tried to wriggle free, but no terror could tear the cloths that held her.

They set her in a boat and rowed out onto the water. It was late, the last of the sun was sinking in the west. Veyjtum grew quiet then, watching the sunset and savoring the colors. She did not feel young any longer. She felt old, sad, and robbed of youth.

They did not stop rowing until they were quite deep, then sat smoking their pipes while they waited for the stars to start twinkling. She could see her own constellation – the Crane – setting on the horizon. Then they bound a weighted rope around her waist and lowered her into the brine.

Before they sent her under the dark sea they thrust a thin reed-pipe between her teeth. The weight of the ropes tugged her downwards, but air came, slow and thin, from the surface through the pipe. Submerged, confined, weightless, unseeing, she floated, and realized that whatever this was meant for, it was not to kill.

Slowly her remaining senses faded, until her body seemed to have been taken from her. She was nothing except a mind floating in a void, and a little corner of a mouth where a thin stream of cold air from the world above stroked her tongue.

Her mind retreated to the world of her childhood: a world of fountains and cobbled streets, of libraries and meticulously clipped palms, a city blooming like a flower on a hill and the scent of fresh-brewed tea lingering in the streets. A world like a delicate mechanical toy, where every part moved in perfect time with every other. A world where the stars were suffused with sublime meanings and bore testimony to the order of the universe.

Like sensation, memory faded. In the lingering darkness, devoid of time and place, she wondered what it meant to go mad. She had lived among the insane in their little neat white huts, but Madness would be something different here. Not a quiet pathetic drooling, lips in frantic motion, beating the skull against the wall. Here it would mean death drunk deeply, whirling skies and blood drenched hands.

She breathed in slow and steady, breathed out through dizzy lungs. As her emotions settled like silt at the bottom of her breast she conceived a hatred higher than mere feeling, and planted it firmly on the throne of her heart; an avenging ghost, floating in an endless sea, with all eternity to take revenge.

⌂

At last they pulled her up like a silent statue and bore her back towards the shore. Her eyes searched the stars with the hunger of starved senses. The pin-prick lights fell into new patterns before her mind and seared themselves on her memory. When they had unbound her she found a little stick and began drawing new constellations on the parched earth. All around the men stood staring. The seer and his apprentice. The women and the warriors. They thought she had been shown an image of their heavens; that their terrible gods had come to her and whispered in the dark. They thought she was their prophetess. The fine white-yellow strands of her hair, brittle as dry straw, encrusted with salt, floated in a ghostly cloud around her face. She became, for them, the sun that eats the stars and all their light.

They took her then from camp to camp, so all could fall and worship at her feet. She sat ever staring out at the horizon, and when night came she would draw the stars out on the ground, and trace secret lines reconnecting them. With the hunger of fanatics seeking mystic meaning, they copied these on bleached hides, and spattered the images with blood to learn the import of her prophecies. She had no interest in this. Her work was in a code, where each star was a letter, and she was writing out the way that she would have to travel, if ever she escaped.

◊

At the third camp, the caves were black and twisted as burned tallow, the rock walls bubbled and broken like a boil. On them the devouring earth was painted, groaning in unholy childbirth, life spurting from her bloodied husk and malformed creatures crawling forth from clouds of ash and smoke. This was the place where the bleeding earth tore open, and the tunnels were her ever-gaping, poorly cauterized wounds. Veyjtum knew, from the libraries of her former life, that it was a volcano. The wounds would run deep, and would branch out in many places. This one was guarded, but another might be free.

She waited until all around were sleeping, then, in the blackness, with a crest of moonlight slinking in at the darkened door, she crawled across the cavern to where she knew the caves twisted deep into the mountain's heart. She stood, feeling the toilsome scrollings of the turbulent stone, felt her way down the passage, going on her toes as she had seen men do when they sneak.

Any other girl would have known if she was followed. Would have heard the pad of feet on stone. Would have listened for voices whispering. Veyjtum did not know how loud a breath could be. She did not know if her feet clattered when they slipped on sharp knives of broken stone. In the darkness, there was nothing seen, and she had lived all her life in silence. There was only the feel of stone beside her in the dark.

She followed the left wall. Eventually, it would lead out, or would lead her ever deeper, until dark and thirst overtook her, and she was swallowed in the monstrous womb of her captor's bloody faith. The walls seemed full of trembling, and the scent of gases breathed from sulfurous wounds. Waves of heat passed by like shadows, sometimes so hot that she felt sure her flesh would burn. Her feet were torn, her lungs complaining. But she was far enough from the camp that she felt sure they would never find her.

She followed the wall for an eternity, until she collapsed. Her body had betrayed her. She sunk to the floor and wept herself to sleep.

⌂

In a blast of flame like the breathing of a dragon she woke and found her skin was blackening away. Red blisters rose angrily along her back, and though she curled in on herself in agony she could not keep her hair from kindling in wisps of painful smoke. Coughs seized her chest, her lungs burned with the strong, acidic fumes.

It passed before it killed her. Choking, with dry lips she breathed in the thick, barely sustaining air. Slowly, with great pain, she struggled to her feet. They were clothed in bags of skin like tight-wet socks, filled with fluid. The moment that she put pressure on they popped, bathing her feet in pain as the outer layer of skin tore free. She could not walk, so she crawled. Her knees had been hugged to her chest and were less burned. Thirst grappled with her soul and again she heard the pounding, though this time she could not decide if it was water or molten rock that disturbed her soundless ears.

It did not matter. The rush of flaming wind had not fled down the path behind her towards the way that she had come. Gases belched from the corridors of the broken earth ever spewed themselves towards the open air. Somewhere down this passage was a way out.

⌂

The water was hot and metallic and tasted like fresh blood. She drank it until she could drink no more. The night air wrapped around her and the moon rose like a scalpel, slicing open heaven's face.

The maps she had been drawing, what they had mistaken for prophecies, resolved with utter clarity in her mind. The constellations shifted, became familiar compass points to show her the way home. She stood, embraced by pain, and turned towards the west.

Everything was guided by those stars. By the feeling of the wind. The telling of the weather. The remembrance of days. A thousand times, by those same stars, she could have found her way back. The sky shifted mathematically before her mind. A different day. A different season. The navigation would not change. She knew it perfectly now. Today it would lead her home, but one day, when she was older, it would lead her back. They had shown her all their secrets, their dark lairs, their camps. All was written on the pages of her memory. And with a civilized army at her back, precise as a mechanical toy, she would one day come and crush them to the last remaining bone.

North Laborian Medicine

· · · · ·

It was a strange thing, not a thing like anything that I had seen before nor like anything that I have seen since, and I almost missed it because I didn't much like the man who introduced us. He was a big man, with hands that were always painting grotesque pictures in the sky, and a nose that had given itself up to drink. He dressed in one of those costumes that is supposed to suggest the opulence and mystery of a distant kingdom: a lot of layers of white and blue with a hat that no man in his right mind would put on his head. Strains the neck muscles. I told him so, and I even showed him how much he had restricted the motion of his head by wearing such a contraption day to day but he was uninterested in the maintenance of his own body. He was only interested in the maintenance of the caravan of monsters that provided him with livelihood.

"You must see this specimen, doctor. You've never seen its like. A true one of a kind. Unique. Completely irreplaceable."

"Cut the patter," I said with the precise measure of patience which professional etiquette demanded, "and tell me why you are consulting me?"

He pulled himself up, raising his chin in a way that made the foolish headdress tip dangerously back on its heels. "I am consulting you because I am told that you are the most knowledgeable man of medicine within two day's travel." He sniffed and looked around my surgery, "I would consult with a man of greater stature if I thought that it would survive the journey to Perseverance."

I could see that I wasn't going to derive any useful medical information from this consultation so I agreed to see the poor creature and named my fee. "I don't promise miracles," I warned him, "these creatures are so nearly destroyed by their vices there's hardly hope for them at all. But I'll come around and take a look."

I'd seen the caravan when it had pulled into

town: a rag-tag of sorry looking vehicles pulled by even sorrier looking nags. All of the wagons had been covered over in burlap to hide their contents, as was required by law, and a great bell was rung to warn people to stay away in case some profane shriek would be heard by delicate ears. Not that it mattered. There were very few who actually heeded my warnings about the dangers of the spectacle, and every year I had to treat half the town for eye problems as soon as the show had passed. Well, I was hardly likely to develop any particular vices merely from exposure to the place. I was, after all, on an errand of mercy and merely plying my trade.

A man in the uniform of the frontier guardsman was standing at the gate to the hastily erected faux-palisade wall that circumscribed the fairgrounds. He was blathering the usual nonsense about how these creatures were not to be gawked at for the sake of idle and disordered curiosity, but rather in order to bring about moral instruction through contemplation of the effects of evil on the body and the soul. Rueful hypocrisy. I tipped my hat to him nonetheless and passed through into the inner precincts.

The caravan was much as it had been in my

childhood. There were the same dreary iron cages suspended just high enough above the ground that the smaller children wouldn't be able to stick their fingers through the bars. The same grotesque music, intended to be mournful and cautionary yet composed to be festive enough that it wouldn't put people off the concession stands. These were huddled together at the far end of the fairgrounds and purported to offer delicacies from the far-off lands beyond the dark forests where the monsters lived. A small museum car housed a collection of masks and there was a tutor present who would instruct the youngest and the oldest in the geography of the places where few men dared to go. Everyone attended the lectures of course and nobody paid them the slightest attention. They were all trying to get a peek behind the curtained cages, at the limbs and occasionally things that weren't very much like limbs that kicked and tore at the thick woolen folds.

The owner of the caravan paraded himself through the thinly scattered spectators, stopping here and there to point to one of the specialties of his collection with pride, promising great things for the moment of the great unveiling. It was still a while away. The story was that the monsters could not suffer the sunlight and men of good will could not see by night. Therefore monsters must be seen only in the brief hours of the twilight or the dawn. The dawn showing was always frequented by small children and I recalled well the day that my own grandmother had dragged me from my bed and bundled me into warm socks and a pair of dew-boots before taking me out to see the horrors from the beyond the wall. The crowd that was starting to form now was older, mostly youths with nothing to do and misty-eyed old men.

I followed. Eventually we came to a small building on the edge of the fairgrounds, the sole fixed structure in the place. It contained a good cooking kitchen and several small administrative rooms. I was led into one of the latter. A small pen had been formed by jamming one of the cage walls in between the door and the side wall and screwing it into place. The windows had been temporarily boarded over, both to prevent escape and to keep prying eyes from peering inside. A bed had been made on the other side of this triangular prison cell and it was on this that the creature sat.

I had expected a monster. I had expected the veil to be drawn back as it was in my infancy and a hideous face to be exposed with a mouth full of a double set of crooked teeth, eyes surrounded with foaming flesh, a nose that had become little more than a raw red cave set lopsidedly in the middle of a puddle of oozing, pasty skin. I expected twisted limbs and knuckles the size of pork hoofs, distended guts, veins that stuck out beneath the skin and that moved up and down within the organisism as if dancing to a frenzied beat.

Instead, a pair of curious green eyes stared at me from a strangely ashen face. The creature was emaciated but clothed, hairless, but symmetrically formed, and it sat in a posture reminiscent of a preying mantis it's long, spindly fingers crossed gently in front of its pointed chin. I would have said that it was no monster at all but an ordinary man suffering from a strange skin disease if it had not been for the growths. I call them growths, that perhaps is not the best word. This will sound incredible, but the creature had roots, or branches. Where it ought to have had hair there was instead a great rash of iridescent green running beneath the skin. It brought one of its hands up and ran it across its skull and I saw that whatever the green substance was, it shimmered under pressure and for a while it held the rippled pattern that it had assumed when it was massaged. This greening of the skin was not quite regular, rather it seemed to come from a series of veins like those beneath the surface of a leaf. They converged on a small opening behind the creatures ear from which there grew a supple, woody stalk like a grape vine. This trailed down the side of its neck and disappeared again beneath the skin just beside the clavicle. Other similar outgrowths were visible at various points around the body and I could see that there were more beneath the skin. All seemed to converge on a strange purse, a sort of pocket of flesh that hung over its back. It regarded me steadily, tapping its fingers together in a strange, frenetic way. There was no rhythm to it, but it didn't seem entirely random either. It reminded me of some other phenomenon but I couldn't quite place it.

"Where did you get it?" I turned to the caravan owner.

He shrugged. "These things come into one's possession."

I checked my temper. Waited. Monitored the pumping of my own blood. Good. Equilibrium was essential. Even these minor variations in the body could lead in time to greater perversions of form.

203

"These things come into one's possession in a regular or an irregular fashion which one is capable of recounting if one wishes adequate medical care to be given. Does one understand?"

He cleared his throat. "It was...rescued from a slaving company."

"Then it isn't a captive from the northern forests?"

He looked nervous. It was illegal to traffic in slaves in North Laboria. Captured monsters were permitted to be shown for the purpose of moral instruction, and they could be caged for the sake of public safety, but if he was including a creature capable of rational intelligence in his spectacle... "It is perfectly monstrous," he assured me. "Simply look at the thing. You have to agree. And it doesn't speak. I've tried every possible means of extracting language from it and to no avail. It is a monster, I'm sure, representing some strange and particular form of vice as yet unencountered. I use it as an example of the originality to which depravities may at time give rise, the need to tutor oneself against even unknown debasements."

"Is it dangerous?" It looked weak, but there was something about the way the thing looked at me that I didn't like.

"So far it has not proved so."

"And what's wrong with it?"

"It doesn't eat. I...acquired it ten days ago. It takes water well enough, and occasionally it nibbles, but in those entire ten days I haven't been able to find a single food that it will endure. I've wondered if it isn't perhaps suffering from an exaggerated sense of culinary delicacy."

Delicacy would have explained the fingers, but in my experience produces a distinctive reddening of the cheek, not this appalling greyness, and certainly no vice within my medical knowledge would have caused vegetable matter to grow within an animal body. "You had better open the cage."

A small iron door was pulled aside and I stepped in. There was barely enough room for me to stand next to the bed and so I was forced to sit down next to my patient. It turned its head ever so slightly and watched me. That curious tapping of the fingers became more pronounced. I reached out to touch the strange growth at its neck. It slid its hand violently to one side, knocking my arm away. The movement was simple, curt, orderly, and then its fingers returned to their irregular drumming.

205

"Please," I said slowly, "I don't want to hurt you." I spoke in a soothing tone. This time I reached in much more slowly, gingerly, hoping to gain its trust. It grabbed my wrist. Its fingers were much stronger than I had expected them to be and they felt as if they were made of pure bone. They clamped down on my wrist and I grimaced in pain. The pressure was withdrawn. I tried without success to pull my hand free. Again the fingers tightened and again I winced. With its other hand it reached out and held my elbow steady, then very slowly and very deliberately tightened its vice-like grip until I cried out in pain. It relaxed. Blinked. Repeated the experiment, only this time not going quite so far. There was no question, it was studying me, evaluating my reactions. I realized that it had positioned the fingers that gripped my elbow in such a way that it would be able to precisely gauge my pulse, the movements of my tendons, the straining of my muscles. I steadied myself, controlling my responses, meeting its eye. There was a shift in its expression and it tightened its fingers again. This time I resisted the impulse to cry out. It continued compressing my wrist-bones until I was sure that they were going to fracture. My entire body was shaking with the effort of self-control. An involuntary groan dodged from my lips. It released me entirely and sat back, its fingers crossed, no longer tapping, withdrawn into its thoughts.

"What are you?" I said, muttering to myself.

"Kss." It made a sound like that, hissing behind its teeth.

"Kss." I tried repeating the sound.

There was a look on its face that might have been very dry amusement, or might only have been my imagination. "Kss." It repeated the sound very deliberately as if it were a schoolmaster teaching a slow student.

I reached into my bag and I took out a slate. I kept it for doing mathematical sums when I needed them in my work: it is one of my faults that I have never been able to keep numbers from falling out of place in my head. I wrote my name on the slate and handed it over to the thing. It took the slate, looked at me with bemusement, and accepted the chalk. Very carefully it drew a series of lines across the slate and began to place little dots between the lines. After each dot, it would tap the chalk on one of its fingers. Eventually I worked out that there was a very straightforward pattern to it. A high dot for the thumb, a low dot for the little finger. I pointed to my own fingers to indicate my understanding. I imagined it looked pleased.

Over the course of an hour it showed me the different patterns that could be made with different combinations of fingers touching the slate, and then showed me how these patterns could be made by touching fingers together in the air as it had been doing since I arrived. I was sure that this was a form of language but I couldn't get the creature to pin a meaning on to any of the permutations of its art. Whenever I attempted to introduce clear referents into the discussion it would look irritated and push them aside.

After a while it handed me back the slate and gestured towards my bag. I replaced the article. It resumed the posture in which I had found it, tapping away merrily to itself and ignoring me entirely. I had no better idea than I had when I'd arrived whether it was in good health or ill. I tried once more to examine the root-like cords that pierced its body, but was rebuffed with the same implacable defenses as before.

I returned the fee for my services to the caravan owner, apologized for my failure, and returned to town.

I admit freely and with a good conscience that it was by my instructions that the creature was seized from the caravan and placed into the care of the local constabulary. There I had it restrained and stripped so that it could be properly studied. I could find in it no evidence that its state had been brought about by vice. It seemed rather to be like the brown men of Narinantia whose bodies are as silent as dumb animals, or the Benai'i who are known to be untrustworthy because they might have a high and noble brow and yet be ignorant and mean. It was not of our species. There was no evidence that it was capable either of the male or the female reproductive function. Its body seemed not to elicit any pain when I manipulated its woody cords. These, so far as I could tell, were indeed of vegetable composition though the rest of the body was perfectly warm and fleshy to the touch. Once it realized that it could not overcome the straps that held it to the table it lay quietly and endured these investigations without complaint, nor when it was released did it attempt to take vengeance of any kind. Indeed if anything it had a sort of supercilious look as if I amused it.

I pointed simply towards my bag and I took out the slate again. This time it began to draw a picture made up entirely of dots. The dots spun out from the centre in a radial pattern complex and mathematically precise. I pointed towards the inmost dot, took my hand, and tapped one of its fingers against one of mine. It pointed to the next dot and did the same. I looked at the drawing with bewilderment. It was clear that it was now moving on to the next stage of learning its language, and the next stage involved a geometric progression expressed in image. In all of my life I had never felt so inadequate as I felt now, fumbling to make sense of what it taught me. I think it sensed my frustration. The lesson was shorter than it had been before. I tried writing a word on the slate and showing it an object. It played the game for a couple of rounds, imitating my markings, but then it gave the slate to one of the guardsmen, took his hand and forced him to write the same word that I had written. "Cup," it wrote with his fingers, and then showed him to hold up the cup. After a few repetitions of this strange behaviour I realized that it was trying to force the guardsman to play the game with me so that we would go off together and leave it alone.

Apparently it attached no more meaning to my writing than I would have attached to a dog with a ball.

I continued to observe the creature's habits. We could find nothing that it would eat, and so it became necessary to take it walking in the woods, constrained by a tether so that it wouldn't escape. After several trips it pulled itself up into a tree and then bent itself over a limb upside down and began to stroke its back. By slow pressure, it evacuated the contents of the fleshy pouch that I had noticed on my first examination. Soil, dry, sandy, evidently depleted. It got down and began to look around on the forest floor until it found a good patch of moist loam and then it filled the sagging pouch. After that, I noticed that it was in the habit always of finding a windowed place and of sitting in the sun. It was a wonder that it hadn't died being dragged about by that dreadful caravan in the dark. I spoke to the mayor and got permission to build it an outside enclosure to improve its health.

We continued with the lessons as we had before but I couldn't make much progress. Different diagrams were tried, different series, but I couldn't imagine how I was going to take these abstractions and turn them into understandable language. There was no sign of particular frustration on the part of my teacher, just a relentless patience that seemed increasingly withdrawn and faintly bored.

One night I woke to the sound of singing. It was more like the song of bird than it was like a human song and at first I lay awake trying to work out what species it could be. I went outside to see and found that my friend was making these sounds. I couldn't reproduce them at all, but thought that they were very beautiful. In the morning, I found that all of the vegetables in my garden had grown prodigiously overnight. The strange being was sitting on the ground in its enclosure and there was a weird sort of smile on its face. I took out the slate but it very calmly put it back inside my bag and went back to tapping to itself.

That night I heard the sound of singing again, but I ignored it and allowed it to lull me to sleep. In the morning when I woke I found a vine growing in my yard. It had sprung up so quickly but its strength had bent the iron bars of the enclosure I had built leaving a gap surrounded in a fringe of greenery. The creature was gone. If it had left footprints, it had sung the grass into growing behind it and there was nothing to indicate the path that it had trod.

WEEPING MOUNTAIN

· · · · ·

No one could say when or how, or in what manner the spirit of the mountain had been offended. Stories abounded: that a herd of mountain goats had once been slain on her slopes and not a single liver promised to quench her thirst for blood; that there was a god chained on the peak of the mountain, above the height where anyone had ever been able to climb, who was woken each year by the roaring of the spring thaw and whose moans were the writhings of his eternal hunger; or that the mountain herself was alive, and pregnant with a giant who would one day rise up and tear the heavens down from their foundations, and that these groans were the pangs of a labor that would not be completed for thrice-three ages of the earth. Belief varied from village to village, from tribe to tribe. We were all agreed on only one matter: that the weeping of the mountain could be quieted only by an offering of innocents.

Thus it was that each spring, the fathers of the village would don masks in the form of a goat, or a vulture, or some vile insect, so that neither their children nor their polished brass mirrors would be able to recognize them, and they would sneak out in the middle of the night. Each tribe would gather at some sacred spot where the blood of rams was thick on the mountain-side and flies congregated to supply the gods with their unceasing music. There they would select a man by a secret means which was never known to us women. Every woman would then see that her husband had left the house in the form of a beast, and she would go to the room of her eldest child, and would lie down in their bed, and would clutch them to her breast and tell them to go to sleep, and that the mountain would soon stop weeping, and there would be no more sorrows to darken their dreams. But the children knew, always knew, and they would get no sleep clinging to their mothers' shoulders in the dark. At last the men would be heard coming home, their footsteps grim and stealthy on the mountain-side, and in some hut there would be a weeping and a wailing to join with the voice of the mountain, and then all of the other villagers would fall back in secret relief, and the mothers would clutch their children to their hearts as though they had just discovered something lost, and some lone, unhappy woman would fall on the floor next to her mat of skins and beat at her breast and tear at her hair and scream for her son until morning had broken itself across the mountains.

Each village did this, and on that night some child, terrified and clawing at the hands of a beast that it did not understand to be its own father – or, perhaps, it did understand, and knew the smell, and the firmness of the paternal grip, or it could see the beard peaking out from beneath the edge of its father's mask. Yes, I think it likely that the child is not deceived, for children rarely are. So it would plead and try to escape, and all in vain until in the coldest hours of the night it arrived weary, sweating like a beaten horse, at the mouth of the cave near the snow-line at the top of the weeping mountain. It is not known, or is not said, or is not spoken of, what is done there, except that the child is never known to return. Mothers say that they can hear when the mountain's weeping intensifies, they can hear the sound of their own child's voice mixing with the groans of the stone. Perhaps it is so. In any case, the father returns, and he takes off his mask and burns it, and he is never, so long as blood flows through his veins, asked to come out on that night again. In the morning he returns to his tent and he says, "Woman, what has become of our son?" and his wife says, with venom in her eyes, "A beast fetched him off in the night. I could not fight it off." And then she treats his wounds with the sharpest vinegars that she can find, and berates him for having abandoned his family on that night, when they most required his protection.

In the morning, the mountain ceases its weeping and the life of the village resumes. Headaches are healed, madness flees from the eyes of men, and ailments of the liver cease to smart. The gardens are watered and the herds give birth. The rivers calm themselves and the fish come upstream from the valleys below. Then we forget, because forgetting is easy, and the mountain hordes up her tears again 'til spring.

Wake Up, You Earth

• • • • •

The ritual outcasting had taken place beside the Pools of Forgetfulness so that once they had turned their backs on Kado, the Queen and people of Naranantia would be able to wash the image of his face from their eyes, and the violence they had done him from their hands.

It was a neat, and civilized violence. A long silver needle with a sharp hook at the end had been slipped down into his ears to pierce the membranes. When it was done, the sound of chanting still rang in the hollows of his skull as though blood and pain could carry a melody.

Apart from that he remembered little except that it was interminable, and that the pain had eventually sufficed to bring him to his knees. The priestesses had offered him the bough of reconciliation then, thinking that the loss of hearing had sufficed to change his heart. In anger and mourning for his ears he had refused. He had been stubborn, but perhaps from something nobler than pride. Still, it did not soften the memory of his mother's back turning away from him: the way that she had straightened her shoulder blades, and the tight, sagging lines of defeat that her posture and her silk robes couldn't hide.

When it was finished they had taken him a long way through dead streets to a strange gap that he had never noticed in the face of the wall. The wall had always looked like an unbroken horizon, a dragon's tail curling lovingly around the nest, or a womb, perfect and impenetrable. Only now as the iron grille creaked open and he was thrust through the dark gap into the outer world did he realize that it had doors.

No one had ever seen the wall from the outside. It was immense, endless, taller than it was from the inside, covered in a shaggy hide of creeping moss, with sharp rows of teeth standing on its parapets. Behind him, away from the wall, where he hardly dared to look, was a thing called a jungle. A tangle of trees and vines. The sinister moral to a story for the wicked child.

He stood dumbly, looking at the closing gate. A margin was kept along the edge of the wall, thin, straggly plants, as though the things of the jungle were ashamed to creep up so close to the bastions of Naranantia. In the grass there sat a crowd of women, nearly naked, with strange marks painted on their faces and beads in their hair. They were shaking things at the wall and raised their hands as though weeping. Outcasts, he realized, like himself. And he wept to think that his own clothing would one day shrivel and rot in the sun, and become so torn that he would have to consent to wear things woven out of weeds, and that his flesh would grow dark and he would become dirty and would have to grub for alien roots.

⌂

Atâ-tupa had come to the wall for her son. She was old-married, and only once a mother, even though eighteen summers had passed through her bones. Her son was three, and they had taken him away. It was only three days ago, and her breasts were still heavy with the milk that she was saving for him. That was why she was here. Because one day the ground was going to rise up and throw down the stones of the wall. Because one day the very ground was going to shake its back, and all those children would come running out into the light. The wall had eaten them for now, but not for forever, and a mother had to be there to cry her tears into the ear of the ground to wake him up.

The mouth of the wall opened. It was a little mouth for such a terrible wall, but its teeth were sharp, and sometimes fire came out of it. Today, a man came out. He had blood coming from his ears, and he was spit out on the grass. He stood there, just like you would expect a man to stand if he had been in the belly of the wall for all those years and then it had spit him out like a bone. He stood and looked at the wall and put his hands on his ears and he cried like a child.

When he had been standing there a long time, and still wasn't moving, Atâ-tupa went over to see if a spirit of wood had gone in through his ears to make him stand so still. "You come out of the belly of the wall," she said, "maybe you know where it ate my son to?" The man looked up and she could see that the spirit of wood had gone in deep, maybe to his heart, and that it had made him dumb. She went over to one of the skin pots that were hanging above the fires. She scooped some stew into an old dried gourd-husk. "Eat while it is hot," she told him, "there is still fire in it. It will burn out the wood." But he didn't hear her. He just fell back on the grass like a log and stayed there, staring at the wall. Atà-tupa got down on the grass beside him, and picked up his head. "You are like my child," she told him, "just like my child." She meant that he had no beard, and that he was smooth and clean, and that he smelled like good things, and that his mind was still empty with nothing to fill it. She stroked his head, and while she did, she beat with her other hand on the ground and said, "You'd better wake up, you ground, before my boy is forgetting everything like this one."

⌂

It was nearly night when Kado realized that he had been staring at the wall for the entire day. There had been a woman, a while back, but she had wandered off. Now she came back, and she was carrying food. He did not think that he would be able to eat. "I'm sorry," he said, and his voice vibrated soundlessly in his skull. "You are very kind." She shook her head and he realized his error: her ears would have been put out too, just long ago, so they didn't bleed anymore. He picked up a stick and cleared a place on the ground where the dirt was shallow, and began to write, but she stilled his hand and shook her head. Her cheeks were as large and broad as coconuts, and her brow just as shriveled, and he was surprised by the expressive elasticity of her features as she showed, with grimaces and gestures, that she did not not know how to read. He nodded and bowed in shame. Of course she could not. She was a woman, and it would have been an insult for her to have to do such demeaning work. He had forgotten the dignity that was due to her, because she wore only grasses and had dead insects woven into her hair as jewels. He looked around for a man who might be her secretary, but there were only the women. She gestured towards the skin pot, and the smell of some rough soup, and the woven blankets. He swallowed his pride and followed her. I have chosen this, he told himself. I could have chosen differently. I could have begged forgiveness, and told them that I was wrong. I had the choice to lie. He had not understood, though, when he had stood and let them put out his ears, that beyond the gates of the city there was nothing.

⌂

There was a sound like the snake moving through the jungle. The great and terrible snake, devourer of lives. The women all knew this sound. They had heard it before, when their children had been taken, and had followed it back to the mouths of the wall. It was a snake of men's boots, and of breasts covered in metal scales.

The snake that was made of men was carrying children again. It closed around them tightly and held them inside of it, but the women could hear the children crying inside, and they rushed forward. Atâ-tupa gave a sharp stone to the man that had come out of the wall, and pointed towards the snake. "See," she said, "you are a man. You escaped from the belly of the wall. Now you have to save these other children." And she picked up a rock and threw it at the snake-men so that he would understand. The wood was still deep in him, though, and he just stared stupidly and dropped the rock on the ground. Atâ-tupa picked it up and joined the other woman. They rushed onto the man-snake with rocks and sticks, and when it was done, many of them were hurt, and some killed. Their blood went down into the ground, and it was sure going to wake him up soon. They could see that they had wounded some parts of the snake, but it had glittering teeth that shone sharper than any knives, and they cut right into a person's flesh like it was made out of squash. Atâ-tupa got one of those teeth in the side of her stomach, and it sure hurt. She made sure that she fed some of the blood to the ground before she bound it up.

When she was all fixed as well as she could be, she looked for the man-child with the wood in his heart. For a long time she couldn't see him, then she saw that he had run right up to the wall, and he was trying to climb in, behind its teeth, and the tail of the snake was pushing him back out. She ran up to him. "You are stupid," she said. "Why are you trying to get back in there?" But for a moment, before the snake had disappeared entirely inside, she caught sight of something glittering in behind the teeth. High, white, shining things, like ranks of tusks or stones for a giant's burial.

⌂

This is the crime for which Kado had been outcast. He was a scribe, to a woman of high estate. Now a scribe is not to remember what he reads. The words pass from the page across his lips when he reads, and through the ears into the hand when he writes. As a pipe no longer holds the memory of

226

water that has passed through it, so the scribe is not to remember the words that have passed through him. He is a man, and knowledge will do him very little good. He will not know how to use it, only how to make ideas out of cloud that have nothing to do with reality. It is because his mind is no good that he is taught to read: because when the mind learns to read, the memory is punched full of holes, like a wall with termites. It can only hold a little knowledge, and then it lets it out. Women's minds are too precious to damage them in this way.

Kado's crime was that he had become curious. He had stopped doing the exercise that cleared the mind so that the lips could speak without understanding. He had ceased to concentrate on the melifluence of the syllables as he spoke them, and when he had knelt down beside the pools of forgetfulness, and had washed his hands in them so that the water would carry away his thoughts into silence, he had trapped the learning in his mind, and had held it there, so that his hands were telling a lie. It was this lie that had been his undoing, for one day, as he knelt in contemplation of a poem that he had been reading for his lady, he had looked down into the waters that were supposed to wash away the lines of verse from his mind, and he had become afraid. It was true that he could not, as the women did, remember the next day exactly what he had read the day before. The words tripped on his tongue, and they came out broken and mangled, no matter how hard he tried to trap them in his mind. But now a terrible thought had come to him: what if this was not because of the inferiority of his mind? What if these pools really did contain forgetfulness, and the women had maintained their secret knowledge by forcing their scribes to wash away the things that they had read? What if the lines of verse that he was still cherishing in his heart would stay inscribed there if only he did not dip his hands down into that pool?

He had kept them hovering over the water, trying to look as though he was washing them, as the lines of the poem washed again and again over his mind. The next day, he had remembered the poetry, and he had vowed that he would never bathe himself in forgetfulness again.

The next day, it had been noticed that he did not put his hands in the pool, and he had been asked the reason. He had not had the good sense to lie.

⌂

"You know, you are going to do yourself no good, staying here forever." Atâ-tupa was trying to explain things to the man-child. "When the men come, you go with them. You go and they will teach you where the hunting is, and how to build a village that the snakes can't find." She was explaining these things with her hands as well as her tongue, because even though she had used the strongest kinds of fire-spice, the wood still hadn't got out of the man-child's ears. "When a woman weeps, it wakes up the earth. When a man weeps, then the ground eats up all his strength. Weeping is woman's work. Men have other work to do."

The men came, but the man-child would not go with them. He stared at them like they were monsters out of the darkness. Atâ-tupa's husband had brought her a good piece of wild pig. She showed it to the man-child so that he would understand that there was meat out in the jungle, and his heart would swell with the pride of being a man. But he only looked sick. She put the meat into a skin pot with some water and some hot rocks to boil it. Then she took her husband and they went into the jungle to try to make a new baby. If there was a new baby, then she would be able to go back to the village, and it

229

would be some other woman's turn to weep and try to wake up the ground.

On the fourth day of his outcasting, the gate of the city opened again. He rushed forward. He was going to explain that he was sorry, and that he had been foolish. He was going to beg them to send him out to break his back in the fields, or to send him down into the darkness to wrest the metals from the earth's breast. He would promise to bathe his entire body in the pools of forgetfulness, and make his life an immolation to Dragon and her wisdom. He was going to ask for the lash, and offer them his hands in reparation. Any disgrace, if they would let him back in.

But when the gate opened, a woman came out. Her face was as hard as stone, and her eyes stared out in front of her as though the pools of forgetfulness were there, behind them. In her arms she held a newborn child. Blood was coming from the infants ears. She placed it on the ground, turned and went back inside. Kado was still staring in horror at the little squirming thing on the ground when the gate shut itself, and he did not have a chance to make his case.

The baby was white. An unnatural color that no human creature ought to have been. There was no down of black on its head, and when it opened its eyes, they were a terrible shade of blue, as though they sky had come down out of the heavens and trapped themselves inside the baby's skull. The child was a girl.

The woman who had been looking after Kado stood up and picked up the crying baby. She wrapped it up in a blanket made out of reeds, and opened her shirt, as though she was an animal and forgotten that she was a woman at all. She squeezed at her breast. There was a little drop of milk, almost dried up, as though the breast was remembering a child that it had lost not so long ago. She put the baby up against it, and the baby began to eat. Kado lowered himself down onto the ground and put his head against the earth in shame. When he rose, he looked at the wall of Naranantia, and he saw it now as the stone body of the dragon, twisting itself along the backs of the hills, her mouth opening with bright teeth to disgorge her children.

When the woman had finished feeding, she tied the baby to her back. She said something to the other women, and they all seemed to agree. They gave her gifts: a colorful wooden bowl, a necklace of seeds, a burning coal from one of the fires. She turned, rejoicing, and set out towards the jungles.

Something wild, inexplicable, and fiercely protective rose up in Kado's heart. Suddenly he felt that this woman could not go alone, with a baby, out into that dark place. He stood, with his loins cramping at the thought of what might be out in that darkness. The woman was waving her arms out around her naturally, and opening her mouth as though she was singing a song. She was not afraid, and he felt ashamed, for her sake, to be afraid himself. For the first time since Naranantia had spit him out, he turned his back on the walled city. Slowly, deliberately, as ceremonially as the city had turned her back on him. He followed the woman out, into the sharp-toothed freedom of the trees.

How It Was

• • • • •

It was how it was. Up in the morning to the sound of the Laborian Anthem of the Dawn being squawked out on a beat-up old crumb-horn. Living in a hut on roots and fish. How it was. Keeping hold of the raggedy shred of *pax Laboriana* out in a rat-hole jungle at the ass-end of Winiuv. Nobody paid you. No one knew or even cared that you were out there. From the day that you were born until the day that you died, living with your neck in the frayed noose of the Laborian dream. That's how it was.

There was only one thing that kept you going. Or rather one thing that kept the old men going with their wet-dreams of Empire. A letter. A rat-licking, snake-suckin' letter that got sent out by the King of Laboria once a year. Not that he probably even wrote

233

it. Not that he probably even knew that it was being written. It was the same every time. "In honour of your great devotion... the service of your forefathers... the inestimable value of your continued allegiance... under difficult and heroic conditions... unfortunate circumstances... special affection and regard for our separated brothers in Empire... kept forever within the gilded precincts of the royal heart... to you and to your sons in perpetuity... a boundless debt... we eagerly await the day when it will be possible to repay..." Stamped with the King's own seal. The snake-sucking seal of a maggot-breathing King. Yeah, well Laborius VIII could lick a rat. The Laborian Empire could lick a rat. The whole snake-sucking, grub-guzzling world could swallow turd and lick a rat. That's how it was.

⌂

The letter hadn't come this year. Wasn't ever coming again. Something to do with trade routes and diplomatic relations. Something to do with the Metenem government feeling threatened by Laborian citizens serving the Laborian King while living on Metenem soil. Apparently 90 years of loyalty and generations of hardship meant less to the King than the price of saffron. Whatever. He picked up his musket. Old junk, leftover from a war that been cold and stale for nearly a century. Perpetual fucking devotion. He oiled it. Not that oiling it helped much. Still, this was one of the better ones. He laid it across his lap and popped a plug of guhtag into his mouth. The only thing that made life in the jungle bearable. That and the occasional Suese girl on a raid.

He had everything that you needed to survive sentry duty. One standard issue Laborian musket, circa grandpappy's birthday. One moth-eaten Laborian uniform, probably older than that. One tin of guhtag plugs. One skin full of watered down poi-juice, slightly fermented, just enough to keep you mellow but not enough to dull your wits. One stupid rat-licking hope that in the far future there would be a King on the throne of Laboria. A man. With bollocks. One who would drive the Metenem out of Winiuv and bestow upon the sons of your sons the recompense that they were promised. With five generations back-pay. Yeah. Right.

The border wasn't much of a border. Not really a border. Just a place in the hills where you could see a long way in most directions. A little pile of rocks that you could hide behind, just in case. Just a pile of rocks that you defended because your fathers had defended it. He settled himself down, laid the musket at his side and leaned back against the hillside. He took another plug from the tin and chewed slowly. Just a place where you could wait it out until you died.

Although he didn't expect it he wasn't exactly surprised by the rabble of cudgel-wielding peasants who wound around the side of the slope. You could only raid, pillage and kidnap people so many times before they decided to do something about it. He was impressed maybe a little that they'd made it so far so quietly. They were now only a couple hundred feet away. Whatever. They didn't stand a chance and there was only a handful of them anyway.

He calmly unshouldered his weapon and reached down to his belt to uncork the powder horn. Most of the rabble were young men: unmarried, nothing to loose, looking for some action. But what was that at the front? A girl?

He dumped some powder down the barrel and pounded in a ball. The rabble was getting a little closer now. Definitely a girl, wielding some kind of club. Probably just a tree branch. Yeah, nothing but a tree branch, probably. No problem. She'll go down like the rest. He'd never seen a wormy girl lead a rabble before, but she was obviously the leader. Odd. The boys'll probably run if I can pop her off. He brought the musket to his shoulder and pulled back the flint lock.

It was hot out. No, like really hot. He had unbuttoned his wool jacket all the way down, revealing a chest and belly reddened with heat rash. The uniforms lost their shape over the decades, but somehow the lice survived. Uniforms made for a completely different climate. Not that he was made for this climate either. True Laborian blood boiled in this heat. He poured a trickle of poi-juice over his face and for a moment the muggy breeze actually felt cool. Above him, a colorful fruit parrot took flight, flapped a couple of times and then landed again on another branch a few yards down, as if pushing the soupy air out of the way with its wings was just not worth the effort. The soldier scratched the irritated skin stretched over his gut and took aim. No rush, lots of time. Wait until she's in range.

The villagers moved towards him slowly, their faces silent with a crackling anger. The girl stared down the soldier, looked right down the barrel of his gun out the back of the chamber and into his eye. And what was that she was carrying?

He pulled the trigger and the flint fell, but the air was so wet the powder wouldn't light. He swore and pulled back the lock again. No rush. It's fine. Lots of time. He stared back at her down the sights of the musket. Something about those eyes, like there's a demon on her back. But it's okay, it's just a big stick. A rat-licking stick.

He stared, losing precious seconds. He broke away from her eyes and pulled the trigger again. It went off this time, but the bullet flew wildly over the heads of his enemies and into the jungle. He realized his hands were shaking badly. He went for the powder horn again. Just a maggot-chewing girl with a stick!

⌂

I raised my eyebrows, a little scandalized. "Grandma, since when do you know how to swear in Winiuvois patois?"

"Don't be silly, Thut. I learned all the bad words from older children when I was a little girl, same as you did. We used them to scare the traders when they thought they could take advantage of us backwards Suese girls in the market. And I can't very well have the soldier in my story talk like a Ptemyen matron at a tea party. Now do you want me to continue or not?"

I took a sip of tea and spoke to the ghost. "Please do. This doesn't sound like it's going to turn into one of your moralizing parables."

"Well, I don't know about that," Grandma Bo sniffed. "But you're right, this is a different kind of story. This is a story that really happened to me. Or at least one that I had a part in. That was just the introduction. We have to back up a bit to get to the part that I'm in."

⌂

I was younger then. Well, not so young I suppose, but your mother was already grown up and off on her own adventures, so I was settling down to a quieter mode of life where young people don't go charging around everywhere mucking up your day. I was out in the jungle looking for gantao blossoms to ease the labour pains of the young wives in the village. When my basket was full and I got back to my cottage I found her there. The poor girl-- she couldn't have been older than twelve-- was hiding behind my sweet pepper plants and munching on my peas. She was all scratched up and covered with insect bites and her eyes were wide like giant red hollows. Eyes that hadn't slept in too long and had forgotten how to focus at anything except the private nightmares forced upon them by the mind.

I stood watching her for a few moments. She hadn't noticed me, but by and by she looked up and was so startled she fell back on her hands. As she scrambled to get up and run away from me, I saw she had a badly sprained ankle and could hardly move.

"My dear, I don't know what those eyes of yours have seen, but I'm pretty sure I'm the least frightening person you've encountered in a long time." She tried to start running and fell down again. "I'm a very un-scary old woman. About the scariest thing I do is serve hungry little girls bean soup made with wild pig hocks." She looked back at me vacantly. "Well, I'll go inside and get the soup warmed up. The door's open so you can come in when you're ready." I could see it was no good trying to help her up. She was like an injured skoo-tail that is ready to bite off any helpful fingers. So I just stoked up my little fire and put the soup on. Presently, she opened the door a crack and stood on the threshold. The smell of cooking meat made her reel a bit. I don't know if you've ever been that hungry, Thut. So hungry that meat seems more solid and real than you are. Like it has more life in it than you do and you wonder who will eat and who will be eaten. I beckoned her in and convinced her to sit on my rocking chair. I noticed she was shivering despite the summer heat and the fire. Fever. I got out my winter blankets and wrapped her in a cocoon of goose-down. I turned to fix her a bowl of soup, but when I brought it over to her she was already sleeping that heavy, dead sleep of those who try not to have any more dreams.

She slept for the rest of that day and on into the next. She half-opened her eyes a couple of times and I managed to spoon a bit of food into her, but mostly I had to let her body try to sort itself out. And her mind. When she was sleeping soundly I walked to the village and traded some mushrooms with one of the men who climbed into the mountains to collect blocks of ice from the glacier. I bound her ankle tight and put the ice on and set about cleaning out her cuts and scrapes. I had never worked on a patient so totally unconscious as she was. It was strange, almost like cleaning a body for burial. But she wasn't dead. She was young and the young have a fountain of life deep within them that is very hard to dam shut. So I let her sleep and watched the waters of life trickle back into her flesh, rising as the tide rises with the moon.

Late in the day after the day that I found her, she awoke. She didn't move, but neither did she fall immediately back into oblivion. "Well, dear, it's good to see you awake." She gave me that same vacant stare. "You can call me Grandma Bo, if you like. What shall I call you?" Nothing. "Don't want to talk, eh? Well, I can understand that. I've got some sticky-bread cooling on the kitchen table. Would you like some?" She turned her head to look towards the table and I handed her a loaf. She tore into the dense, moist bread, shoving handfuls into her mouth. After only a few bites she began to choke and cough as she tried to swallow the huge chunks. I got her a cup of water and patted her on the back, but as soon as she had stopped choking she began to eat as fast as before.

◊

A couple of days went by and she still didn't talk. She ate and slept a lot. Food and a warm bed are the most potent herbs in a grandmother's medicine chest and are usually the only things that children need to get better. I didn't know who she was or where she was from, but she'd let me lay her head on my lap as I stroked her hair and make soothing noises as if she were an infant.

Within a few more days, she was up and walking around with only a slight limp. She refused to go outside, but was happy to help me around the cottage. Someone from her previous life had taught her how to sew and she was pretty good at it so I let her work through the pile of mending I had set aside for rainy days. I saw that a little, just a very little, of the death had gone out of her eyes.

She handed me a dress she had just lengthened for one of the village girls who had grown out of it and then turned quickly to go on to the next sewing project. I stopped her with a hand on her shoulder. "My dear, there's something you and I have to work out." She didn't look at me. "You know you're welcome to stay here as long as you need to. And if you don't want to talk, I guess you don't have to. Not everyone knows how to talk. Some children are born simple and never talk, but I don't think you're simple, are you? No you're one of those people who have seen something so horrible that they're afraid if they put words to it it'll happen again. You're hoping that if you just don't feed the thing words, it will eventually die. But it won't will it?

Words are like a pretty mobile hanging over a baby's crib. Good as far as they go but... well you don't hang a mobile over the crib of a dead child. You saw an infant, a little girl, die in her crib and since then you've just stayed in that nursery hoping that if you keep picking up that dead child and cooing over it enough it will come back to life.

⌂

I was wide-eyed again. "Grandma Bo... what... what are you talking about?"

The wrinkled old ghost scowled, not so much at Thut, but because telling this story made her irritable. "That's why I tell you parables, Thut! When I try to tell you something straight all of a sudden you haven't a clue what I'm talking about!"

"But..."

"Do you want to know the moral of my story? Everyone goes around with nightmares locked inside their guts and they think they have to lock shut the gates of their minds so that the nightmares don't come out and turn real. But, philosopher, what you haven't learned is that there's nothing more solid than your guts and the nightmares are never more real than when they're in your head, feasting on silence."

244

"But Grandma, what does this have to do with me? And where does the dead child fit into it?"

"That's two questions in a row, Thut. Don't you remember our rule?"

I sighed, frustrated and feeling like a child. "Only one question in a row."

"Right, so which one do you want to ask?"

"I'm just trying to understand what you're talking about. Did the girl see a dead infant, is that what got her upset?"

"There was no dead baby, that was just a metaphor. Besides, by the time a Suese village girl is ready for marriage she's already seen half a dozen infants who have died of the pox. It's one of those things that crush women's hearts, but that men are totally unaware of. Especially men from Ptemya. So pour yourself another cup of tea. It will give your lips something to do other than interrupt me."

⌂

The tide inside her reached up to the rising moon, rising to an impossible crest, teetering to the breaking point in a frothing wave that scraped the bottom of the ocean. It broke as if over a cliff and came flooding out her eyes as violent sobs and wails spilled out. There were no words yet, but the nightmare was beginning to come out. The sobs were it's vanguard. There was nothing I could do but hold the child tight until the tide ebbed. "Pneuoa. I am Pneuoa."

Pneuoa never did tell me what had happened to her, but as the days and weeks went by she began to talk more and more. Not about herself, but at least we could chit chat about the birds outside and the warm sunshine and my sweet peppers. She told me she was from a village up north near the border with Winiuv, but wouldn't say more than that.

Now here's the part where you find out what a selfish old woman I am. She'd been with me more than six weeks and was restored to health. She was slowly healing on the inside too, but was still in many ways like a child. She would follow me around everywhere and get scared when I went out, but would refuse to go into the village. When I had a visitor she would hide in the herb shed until the person left. Well, I knew it couldn't go on like that. I had just got my own children out of the house and wasn't so keen on having another one. If the stars wanted me to play mother to this orphan then I supposed I would have to do it, but it really didn't seem to be the best thing. Not for me and not for Pneuoa either.

⌂

I tried to broach the subject of where she should go next, but it didn't go well.

"No, Grandma Bo, I want to stay with you forever. I won't be in the way and I can help you with all your gardening and sewing and laundry and..."

"But I don't need any help with all that, Pneuoa. There are lots of families around with children your age who could give you a good home. It's not good for a young girl like you to be hanging around a tired old woman all the time. It will turn you into a tired old woman before it's your turn."

"Don't make me go. Please"

"I'm not going to make you go anywhere. It's just that..." I could see I wasn't going to get anywhere and so I let her be. I knew I had to do something a little more extreme, so after a few days of careful planning, I faked my own death.

⌂

"You did what? Didn't that send the poor girl completely over the edge? What were you thinking?"

The ghost of Grandma Bo counted out my questions and held up three bony fingers. Duly chastened, I took a sip of tea. "I'm not as foolish as you seem to think Thut. Of course I didn't just collapse on the kitchen floor and let the girl fend for herself. I had a much more subtle plan."

⌂

I sat Pneuoa down one evening for a talk. "I'm not well, child. I know I look fine, but I can feel it in my gut. Nothing's moving right down there. I don't expect you to understand at your age, but trust me, for someone at my age, discernment of bowel movements is a surer form of augury than reading entrails."

"But you must have a medicine for it. You have a medicine for everything."

"Everything? Do I have a medicine to take the dead out of their coffins or the stillborn back into the womb? Do I have medicine that will take the monsters out of children's dreams?"

"I didn't mean that."

"No medicine has ever cured anyone. The body does its own healing. Medicines just give it enough time to do what it needs to. But yes, as you say, there is a medicine that could help. The trouble is I haven't got any. I need some jhagjub weed, but it only grows high in the mountains north of here."

"Can't you send someone to get it?"

"Someone? Like who? Some village boy who doesn't know where it grows or when the leaves are most potent, or the difference between it and common dwarf fern that is completely useless for anything? No I have to go myself. Or, rather, we have to go ourselves. I'll find the herb, and you keep my rattley bones moving."

So Pneuoa and I headed north into the mountains. Now you don't know about these mountains, Thut, even though you think that you are a very wise and well-traveled fellow who knows everything that there is to know about the world. You have only been to the nice parts of Winiuv, the western ports where a half-Metenem half-Suese philosopher can buy dates and *piama* in the market and no one will trouble to throw a rock at his head. You have not been to the back-end of the province, where it butts onto our land. In those parts they would tie you up in the swamp and take bets on how long you could not die of gag-fly bites. They would hang you up in a tree like a flag and let you blow there until the meat fell from your bones. It is a world of men who fought for something so hard that their sons and the sons of their sons have never been able to let go of it. So they hide in the jungle and they very slowly poison themselves from the infested waters of their dreams. They would like to go and march on your city, but there are not enough of them, so instead they prey on little Suese villages and quiet their consciences by telling themselves stories of Suese traitors selling out to Myetoa.

Now you know how it is with old women: we have roots that go far into the ground which can sense even the secrets that men try to hide under the soil, the way that naughty little boys hide frogs under their beds. I knew that we were treading on some of the paths that Pneuoa had taken in her flight weeks earlier but I feigned ignorance. I could tell that she was uncomfortable going back towards her old home but I ignored her hesitations. In fact I was counting on them. I used her nervousness as a compass letting her unwittingly lead me to where she dreaded most to go. There are only a few passes over the Suese mountains, and there were two in particular where silence had come to roost.

I had been feigning infirmity while all the while trying to keep us moving as fast as possible, but as the jungle thinned and we moved to higher altitudes I no longer had to do much pretending. We had been traveling for five days and I was approaching my limit, so when we reached a sheltered cliff face high in the mountain pass, I was all-too happy to enact the second part of my plan, which involved me taking a good long rest.

Abruptly, I sat down and curled myself up into a hollow of rock. "Grandma Bo?" she asked.

"I'm not going any further." I said, perhaps more grumpily than I intended.

"But you must! We must get the jhagjub weed to make you better."

"I am an old woman!" I shouted to the mountain with great conviction. Pneuoa was a little startled. "I'm old and my bowels are in sustained revolt and I will not take another step! I'll just crawl into this hole and die!"

"But Grandma, you can't leave me!"

"I've got old woman's disease! You'd better go. It's catching!"

"Is there nothing I could do to help?"

"Oh, if you can find some jhagjub weed, I might be able to get myself back on the mend."

"I know, but I don't know what it looks like or where it grows."

"It looks like dwarf fern only it isn't. Now run along and go find some if you want to help." I looked her in the eyes, eyes that were full of passion but still dead. "Don't get lost."

⌂

Don't get lost, stay on the paths that you know. She knew this path. It was a waterfall of rubble spilling down into the jungle. A waterfall she had climbed almost two months ago, running for her life. Jhagjub weed. There must be some down here. I remember passing some on my way up. I think it was Jhagjub weed...

⌂

"Grandma Bo, Jhagjub weed is just a moderately effective constipation remedy and is as common as grass in your part of Suo."

"Yes, but not in the north, so I knew she wouldn't know it. In any case it doesn't grow in the mountains. But I was hoping she would find something else. I let her go for a little bit and then started off behind her, easily following her trail. Your Grandma Bo is like an old nanny mountain goat when she wants to be. I was tired, but I had had a little rest and it was no trouble to keep up with her before her trail got cold." Thut gave her a skeptical look. "A mountain goat. As graceful as a mountain goat am I." Grandma Bo cackled to herself.

⌂

The girls ran up the mountain path. Somewhere behind them, hours of running behind them, the world burned. The whole village, everywhere they had ever been, burned by bored Winiuvois guerillas. There wasn't much worth taking, hardly even any slaves worth hauling down to the black markets of Antjou. But, hell, if you're going to stay up all night raiding a village you had to get *something*. The men were staking claims on everything and everyone that hadn't been reduced to ashes. Two maidens fleeing into the mountains. Hell yeah, that was worth it.

The soldiers caught up with them half way up the hill that led to the pass. Pneuoa and her friend, Ksiera were exhausted, their rib cages heaving in and out with giant breaths. There was no more running. It was just them and the soldiers. Two against two.

"Keep going Ksiera, just a little further."

"I can't."

"The sun has gone down, we can hide in the caves."

"I can't."

◊

An old shaggy wolf let the nighttime smells
waft into his lungs. Fresh kill. Hardly touched. The
soft, easily swallowed flesh of a child. He bounded
from rock to rock, anxious that nothing would get
there before him. He had his own trails through the
mountains, ones the humans were too clumsy to use.
Jump. Jump. And he was there, looking over the dead
child. The metallic smell of blood, still flowing,
overwhelmed him. No animal had done this. An
animal would have eaten her after the kill and he
would have been left with only a few bones to pick at.
No, this was murder. A child run through with a
sword and left where she fell on a mountain path.
She lay on her front, her head twisted brutally to the
side and her clothes torn. Her dark Suese hair was
soaked in blood. The night listened patiently to the
sound of crunching bones and the groans of animal
pleasure.

◊

The cave smelled as though an animal lived in
it. Pneuoa didn't think about what kind of an animal.
She didn't think about what the soldiers were doing
to her friend out there. She shut up her ears with her
fingers and she began to babble to herself very

quietly, very quietly, quieter than a mother's heartbeat. No words. Words would bring thoughts and thoughts would bring knowledge and knowledge...

She bit her lip. The taste of her own blood silenced her tongue for a moment and she could hear Ksiera out in the darkness struggling with the bandits. One against two. Her hand clasped around something in the darkness. She couldn't tell what it was, whether it was a polished piece of driftwood or an old piece of bone, but it would have made a good club. It was solid. Her fingers ran over it like water over a stone. One against two out there. But now the men were distracted. She could even out the odds.

There was a scream and the sound of one of the men swearing loudly. They were words that Pneuoa had never heard before but she could hear what they meant just by the way that they sounded. The voice was so loud and cruel. Fear pinned her insides like a hook. She stuck her fingers into her ears again and began to sing-song to herself. No words. Just the dark and the smell of an animal and the sound of her voice jabbering inside of her own head. Just the feel of that thing that probably just an old piece of wood, running her fingers back and forth over it like a child playing with its mothers hair. One against none until everything outside was quiet and it was too dark to see the nightmare. She rested her head on a stone and shook while the death of her friend played itself again and again in a thousand variations behind eyes that had refused to know.

⌂

The Winiuvois soldier lifted the musket again. She hadn't flinched, not even a little bit, when he fired. Just a damn girl with a stick. A stick and a nightmare in her eyes. Moving slowly towards him, like a glacier sliding down a mountain, like a prowling she-wolf. I'm the one with the musket. I just have to hold it steady long enough. She was only a few paces away from him now. Her eyes seemed to shine in the sunlight, drawing him in. What was in those eyes? Hatred? Death? A hot geyser of life gushing from some cthonic darkness.

He pulled the trigger again. The rifle jumped in his hands and fell to the dirt. Goddam Laborian muskets, left behind at the end of the goddam Laborian war. The bullet kicked up a bit of dust at her feet. Without a word, she and her platoon of villagers charged towards him, suddenly galloping at top speed. She fixed his eyes, old, tired. Eyes spent in the endless service an Empire that had forgotten him and his people. Scratched them from the Imperial ledgers. Abandoned them beyond the scribbled edge of its frontier where it lay sprawled out like a drunk on the map of the known world. She raised that stick. That funny stick with the knobby end. That stick with bits of dried gristle still on it. The soldier's skull crunched under the impact.

Pneuoa had expected to find her friend lying where she had been killed. Had expected the whole scene to play out exactly as it had when morning had come and she had crawled out of that hollow in the rocks. All that was there were a few scattered bones. Wolves and bears had carried most of them away. In fact the only recognizable piece of Ksiera left was her left femur. A long heavy bone with a knobby hip socket at one end. Pneuoa knelt and stared at the bone for a long time as the day faded. Suddenly, the voice of an old woman came from behind her.

"Let the nightmare escape, Pneuoa."

She turned. "Grandma."

"It wants to come out. That bone is as real and as solid as anything. Let it come out. Let it take flesh."

THE WISDOM OF THE MOON

• • • • •

"Grandma Bo?"

"Yes Thut."

"You ought not to wear feathers in your hair. It's ridiculous."

"When I was a girl, every young lady had to have feathers. I had a beautiful blue one, plucked from the tail of a macaw by a boy who thought that I had beautiful shoulders. Someone told me it would bring me good luck in marriage – and it did. I had three wonderful husbands, and they all managed to get themselves killed before they became tired of me or ran off to live in the wilderness."

"Yes. You've told me that. Still, I think vanity in a dead woman is absurd."

"Well, when you are dead, you can wear old bones and misery. I will have my bright blue feather and my throat-lace, just like in life."

Why was she here? When I had come to this little clearing, where her ruined cottage perched at the foot of Old Grandpa Mountain, I had expected to be alone.

"Grandma?"

"Yes?"

"Did your star go too? I thought I saw it last season." Overhead, I could see the hollows in the darkness where the constellations had lost their stars, like old coats whose buttons have fallen off: The Old Woman's Purse, The Greater Mill-Race, The Peacock's Egg, The Tip of the Monkey's Tail.

"Ah ha ha. The old Dragon won't ever gulp my star down. I've got it fixed with my eye – I'll go to it when I'm ready."

"Some would call that heresy."

"The stars will overlook a great deal of heresy in an old woman with such a beautiful feather and such an impious grandson."

"I couldn't find your grave."

"Good. You'd just go rattling my bones with insincere prayers and drown all the flowers. Keep the drive swept for me and I'll look after my own grave."

"The house is gone, you know."

"That's no excuse for leaving a mess on the drive. The horses will get macadamia shells caught in their hooves."

"It's a long time since there were any horses."

"Do you think there are no beasts among the dead?"

I picked up the palm-frond broom. The "drive" was a stretch of overgrown pea-gravel, distinguishable from the surrounding forest only because it resisted the larger trees and welcomed only ferns and tropical nettle. I absently battered the heads of the delicate leaves with the uneven bristles until all the greenery bowed down before me like mocking courtiers before a new-crowned fool. The nettles tore at my ankles in spite.

"The drive is swept," I declared, and sat down to build a fire and brew tea. My tea-set was the only thing in the clearing that suggested civilization. The little cottage where my grandmother had died nearly half a century ago had long since surrendered to the roots of mango trees and the thunder of monsoons.

There was a small, stone door and a half-collapsed root-cellar, given over to mildew and floods. I had hidden all my books down there in the hopes that worms and termites would come to divest me of the burdens of learning.

"Grandma Bo," I said when the tea-pot had boiled. "Would you tell me a story?"

"I would like the cup with the peacock, if you will."

She was being kind: she knew that I hated peacocks. I poured a cup of tea for me, and set out an empty cup for her. It is a kindness to remind the dead of pleasures past, and cruel to set before them drink that they cannot sip.

She ran her fingers along the bony edge of the peacock cup as though she was thinking of bringing it to her lips. "All right," she said, "I'll tell you a story."

◠

Once, there was a little boy who was going to be a philosopher. Now, his father had taught him that wisdom is very shy of classrooms, and skittish with pedants, so the boy decided to go out into the world and see what there was to see. He soon found out that the world was full of terrors, so he came running back home.

-- What sort of terrors? (You had always to be careful with Grandma Bo's stories or they would quickly turn into morality tales and end prematurely. You had to be like a spear-fisher: very watchful, and quick with your questions.)

Oh, so you want to know that, do you? You must be very brave. Well, the first thing he encountered was a woman. She was kneeling by the side of a very ancient river and she was bent over, with her hair trailing in the water so that you could not tell which was which; you see, her hair was black, and the river was black. She had a little basket that was leaking light and golden dew, but when the Philosopher came near, she clutched it very tightly to her breast and wouldn't let him see.

-- What was in the basket?
It was full of stars. This woman was Mother Moon, who gave birth to all the lights of the heavens. But now she is plucking the stars out of the sky and secretly gobbling them up -- her own children -- because she had lost all of her light in giving birth.

-- Which is why the ancient Suese made human sacrifice to the moon.

Before you Metenem came and civilized us. Yes. But don't forget, you are half-Suese too.

-- I glanced down at my hands. They had once been pale. The color of weak-tea, my mother always said. But the sun had been merciless with my Suese heritage and I was now as dark as any full-blood Metenem. I looked up at the sky. Metenem stars with Metenem names. Your Philosopher came upon the moon devouring her children...

Yes, but he did not know her for who she was, and he thought that she had wisdom hidden in her basket. What else could she have treasured so fiercely against her breast? So he said, "Give me wisdom and I will be your servant. If you say I should wake, I would wake. If you say I should fast, I would fast. I shall follow you, for you hold all the secrets in your heart."

The Moon considered this. She had seen many things, and known many things, but she had not known happiness. "Good," she said. "The first thing I require of you is marriage. You shall be my husband, and I your wife, and you will find all knowledge in the meeting of our flesh. But you must swear to me this: the children that spring from my womb are mine.

Perhaps I shall give you one son as an heir, but of the rest, you must never ask."

This request was very startling to our hero, as you must imagine. But he was a Philosopher, so he knew nothing of women, and he agreed. For seven years he lived with the Moon. Seven times she waxed and waned, but the Philosopher knew nothing of the children that had sprung from her womb, until, one day, he came upon her bending over the river and nursing their seventh child -- a daughter. The Philosopher saw the curve of the nape of the baby's neck, and he fell in love: he must have his little child and hold her and be to her as a father ought to be. He went to his wife and told her that all wisdom is as nothing if a man does not know his own children, and beseeched her to show him the little ones she had borne, asking why he never heard their laughter on the wind or saw their footprints running here and there in the mud?

The Moon became very angry, and her face grew dark, and for a long time she refused to say anything, reminding the Philosopher of his promises, but he was not to be deterred. At last she said, "There, since you would wrest a woman's most awful secrets from her breast: seven times have I waxed, and given birth in pain, and not one little one survived into the world. Every time, death has come haunting around my womb, and has carried them off before the first breath." And then she refused to speak to him at all, out of anger that he had pressed her about the matter. But he had seen her nursing a little girl, and knew that she was lying. Still, what else was he supposed to say?

He decided that he would have to follow her, and see where it was that she put the baby to sleep, so that he would be able to sneak down and hold his daughter, and perhaps he would find his other children there as well. So he waited until it was drawing towards evening, and he followed his wife when she went down to the river. She sat by the river-side and he saw her open her mouth and out of it came the little baby that he had fallen in love with. She cradled the child, and allowed it to nurse at her breast, and then, when the girl had finished, immediately swallowed her whole again. It was then that the Philosopher understood: when his wife spoke, and seemed so full of wisdom, it was because the voices of all of his children were there inside of her, for she had never been willing to let them out.

So the next night, the Philosopher waited by the side of the river where the Moon would come to feed her child. He waited until she had taken the baby into her arms, but had not yet put it to her breast, and then he stirred up some fish to jump and swim furiously upstream so that all the flashing of their fins would be a distraction to the mother, then he snatched up the baby and ran. He ran over hills, and through fens, and across rivers full of raging currents, and everywhere the Moon pursued him, howling that he had stolen what was hers. But when day came, the Moon grew tired and could pursue him no longer. He found a cave in the side of a great cliff, where even the Moon would not be able to find him, and he hid himself away inside and looked at his infant daughter. She was beauteous beyond all beauty, and there was the light of the stars in her eyes, and she smiled to see the world spreading around so far above her, for even when she had been nursed at the breast of the Moon, her mother's hair had spread above her like a cocoon and she had seen and known only Mother, and nothing else of the world besides.

He nursed her on the nectar of wild-flowers, and fed her on dew and honey, and she grew, as children do, until she was a beautiful child of five years old. From her babblings, he learned every secret of a father's heart, and he loved her beyond rubies or kingdoms or libraries full of books. During the day, she was free to go and play with the butterflies, whom she had named, and who were, to her, darling friends. She did not know it, but she had given them the names of her sisters, which she remembered, though only dimly, from the time that she had shared with them inside the Moon. During the night, however, he made her come inside the cave, and tucked her up in a bed of silk which the moths had spun especially for her. Then he told her that she must never, if she lived until she was a hundred and three, go out of the cave at night, or something terrible would happen. She asked "Why" and "Why" again, but he would tell her nothing more than that.

It is was in her fifth year that she asked him what the light that came and played on the lip of the mouth of the cave at night was. He told her that it was a dangerous and terrible light, and forbade her to ask about it again. The next year, she wanted to know why the little birds and the tamarins had both a mother and a father, but she had only one. He told her that she had been born of the dew of the flowers, and that all the earth was her mother, and strictly forbade her, again, to leave the cave at night. But when she was seven, he was leaning over a page of poetry that she had written for him during the day, and was absorbed in wonder at the beauty of her words, when she, seeing that her father was well distracted, decided that she would take just a little look beyond the edge of the cave. She stole up to the threshold and ducked her pretty black head just a little outside, and she could see a bright, mysterious glow rippling on the currents of the stream. Fascinated, she took another step, and she could see two dark eyes staring down at her from a pale, pale face up in the heavens. This face was so strangely familiar that she had to have a closer look. She took a last step, completely outside of the cave, and at last saw the face of the Moon. Her father looked up, just at that moment, but there was nothing to be done. Faster than the twinkle in the eye of a star, the child was gone, swallowed up again, and though he went out and fell on his knees and begged the Moon to give her back, his old wife was full of spite, and would not speak to him a single word, or listen to anything he said.

So, you see, this is the first of the terrors that the Philosopher encountered when he went out into the world. Do you think that after this he was ready to return home, or did he need to go on and find more?

♤

"Did he pursue his daughter? Hunt the moon down in her lair? Tear her open and release his children?"

"Oh no, he didn't do any of that. I think he is still waiting for an idea to come to him. A way of letting them free."

"Perhaps. Maybe he's lost hope."

"Oh yes, that's certainly possible. But then, maybe he will find it again. Men sometimes do you know. Your father, I think, was like that. He lost hope in you, and then found it again, before the end."

"How would you know that? You were dead."

"He's over by the well right now, throwing in stones and praying for you. He's waiting for his star to come back into the sky. He can't leave until it does."

"I'm sorry, Grandma. I can't fix the holes in the sky. I can't go home and give up on the terrors of the world. I can't even 'live happily and eat hot buttered cake every morning and every evening' like people in your stories used to do."

"Living happily is not so difficult. I think, right now, if I had a nice plate of salted radishes and some sour plum wine, I could live very happily indeed."

"You couldn't live."

"No, but I dare say there are some ginger roots still left over-growing in my old garden, and if you wanted to you could pull them up, and I could tell you a very good recipe for making beer out of them."

"And I could live happily? With the holes in the sky and my father waiting by the well and my daughter swallowed up by the moon."

"Well, perhaps not. But that's because you never pursued her to the end of the world or cut her open and pulled all the stars out of her belly. There are happy endings, and there are tragedies, and it all depends, in a story, on when the hero gives up."

"And in real life?"

"You are saying that stories are not real life? Oh, you've forgotten a great deal since you were a little boy catching frogs in my garden."

⌂

The Philosopher went home. He found a human wife, and married her, and they had a great many children who frolicked in the meadows, by day or by night, and never dreamed of being swallowed or of being afraid. But he did not live happily. The wisdom that the moon had given him was of a terrible sort. It had planted itself in his heart and grown up like a malignant flower that twisted its thorny vines around his throat and stopped it up so that he could not speak. His wife knew nothing of the moon, or his lost daughter, but he could think of nothing else. What was the laughter of these human children, if it was not filled with the light of the stars? And so he was filled with sorrow.

At last, he could not bear living in this silence. He picked himself up and he went away to live in the wilderness, where he could choke down loneliness and look up at the moon, dreaming of a time when he would find a knife sharp enough, and a ladder high enough, that he would be able to climb to the heavens and cut the heart out of death so that it would release to him the child that it had swallowed. But death is merciless. She does not give back what she has taken. If a man will not be happy with the living, he shall live unhappily indeed.

◬

"Another of your morality tales. I should have been quicker."

"Go home, my little grandson. Run along, back to your wife and children. Leave an old dead woman to tend her own drive and grave and to look after the child that you have lost. When your little one is grown into a woman, I will give her my blue feather. She doesn't weep, you know, and she is still filled with laughter, and when the stars have come back into the heavens, she will have a home and she will know you. All the secrets that you have growing in your heart."

I looked towards the old root cellar. My notes were there, the book that I had been trying to write, the self-revelation that would unlock the world of salted radishes and hot-buttered cake. "Perhaps," I said. I picked up the tea-set and took it over to the well. If my father had been there before, he was not there now. I could see the moonlight trapped in the bottom of the well. I picked up a stone and threw it in, watched it shatter the belly of the moon, but she quickly gathered herself up and was whole again. Death, undisturbed by stones and prayers. I drew up a bucket of water and sat in the moonlight, washing the tea-stains from my cup while the nettles of the overgrown drive brushed against my ankles and termites climbed up out of the dark and secret places in the earth to eat away the secrets that I had hidden in my grandmother's cellar.

About the Author

Melinda Selmys raises children, chickens and vegetables on a small hobby farm in rural Ontario. The ghost of Elvis lives nearby. She blogs at patheos.

Her other books are:

Against Nature and Other Abominations

Eros & Thanatos

Slave of Two Masters

Sexual Authenticity: An Intimate Reflection on Homosexuality and Catholicism

Sexual Authenticity: More Reflections